THE
BELL
AT
THE
END OF A ROPE

OTHER BOOKS BY ABBY FRUCHT

STORY COLLECTIONS

Fruit of the Month

NOVELS

Snap
Licorice
Are You Mine?
Life before Death
Polly's Ghost

THE BELL AT THE END OF A ROPE

STORIES *by* ABBY FRUCHT

NL
NARRATIVE LIBRARY

A first edition from Narrative Library

Copyright © 2012 by Abby Frucht

All rights reserved. Except as permitted under the U.S. Copyright Act of 1976, no part of this publication may be reproduced, distributed, or transmitted in any form or by any means, or stored in a database or retrieval system, without the prior written permission of the publisher.

These stories, some of them in different form, have appeared in the following magazines: "Two Straight Women Talking," *Village Voice Literary Supplement;* "Edwinka Brunhilde," *Indiana Review;* "Is Glistening," "Rehearsals," and "Choir Practice," *Narrative* Magazine; "But You're Not" and "Tamarinds," *New Letters;* "Wingdings" and "Old Inn Door," *Gargoyle;* "McGuffey's Third Eclectic Reader," *Memorious;* "Broken Map," *Controlled Burn;* "Quint," *Silk Road;* "Erasures," *Serving House Journal;* "Frankie D," *Glimmer Train;* "The Empiricist," *Ontario Review.* The editors who helped me at those magazines—Stacey D., Erasmo, Danit Brown, Robert Stewart, Richard Peabody, Rebecca Morgan Frank, Carol Finke, Kathlene Postma, Duff Brenna, Susan Burmeister-Brown, Linda B. Swanson-Davies, Joyce Carol Oates, and Raymond J. Smith—as well as this book's first editor at Narrative Library, Alexander Landfair, were generous in their wisdom, their enthusiasm, their kindness, their technical know-how, and their advice.

Thanks too to Deborah Schneider, the Council for Wisconsin Writers, Vermont College of Fine Arts, and the Edenfred Resident Fellows Program. Laurie Alberts—dear collaborator—is the best of readers, teachers, colleagues, friends, writers, and cheerleaders. Alex and Jess, you are my heroes. Chuck, you are Chuck. And to Joshua Clark, Lacy Crawford, Mimi Kusch—smartest, kindest, most fun, hardest-working editor ever—Tom Jenks, Carol Edgarian, and all others at *Narrative,* these thanks aren't enough.

NarrativeMagazine.com

ISBN 978-0-9843816-9-2

Cover and book design by Miller360

Please direct any questions or comments to:
editors@narrativemagazine.com

FOR ALEX, JESS, AND CHUCK

> I used to say there is another world,
> and it's this world.
>
> —PETER STRAUB

CONTENTS

1.

WINGDINGS   1

BROKEN MAP   26

IS GLISTENING   38

ERASURES   61

QUINT   68

TWO STRAIGHT WOMEN TALKING   74

BUT YOU'RE NOT   91

2.

EDWINKA BRUNHILDE   111

THE EMPIRICIST   120

REHEARSALS   130

OLD INN DOOR   152

FRANKIE D   157

CHOIR PRACTICE   179

MCGUFFEY'S THIRD ECLECTIC READER   195

TAMARINDS   202

1.

WINGDINGS

Years after my sister and I were each married and divorced, had turned practically forty, and had moved to antithetical parts of the country, our parents called me to suggest, in something other than their usually imperturbable style, that I visit Soonie in New York City. Such a visit wouldn't be overdue. We visited regularly back then. But this was different. Soonie appeared to be having an attack of nerves, our parents said to me.

"Attack of nerves! Attack of nerves!" I imagined us sisters shouting at each other, clawing the air in a parody of our parents' quaint vocabulary, our bathrobes fluttering like action-figure capes.

But in the midst of my amusement, part of me stayed quiet, urging our parents on. It wasn't like them to call with a problem. It wasn't like them to *have* problems, period. But it seemed there might be something bothering Soonie and that maybe I'd be able to calm her down. It would do her good to have the company of her sister for a weekend, our father added. We could style our hair together, our mother suggested reasonably, for we often tried out new "buns," as our parents still insisted on calling them, or shopped for eccentric accessories at Bumble Bumble Salon. Once, we'd braided our heads together and gone to a party. In our strapless dresses, with the single, ropy braid between us, we looked like a Chinese finger trap. We had been a big hit, as you might expect, and had ended the night in a far messier entanglement than was made by our looped coiffure. I maintained a competitive friendship with my ex-husband, Leo, a set designer, and when I told him about the men whose various appendages had needed to be pulled clear of Soonie's and mine, and how I couldn't tell her juice from my cream, sometimes, and how my nipples once turned out to be hers and vice versa, Leo only gazed dispiritedly at the crotch of my jeans, as if inside them was his childhood neighborhood, dilapidated now but grand when he had lived there.

"I'll fly to New York next Friday," I promised our parents. I was managing Riverside Condos then, and though I didn't have much work lined up for the coming weekend I was expected to greet a new tenant, a Department of Natural Resources frog specialist or something, whose telephone manners were so croaky and jumpy I dreaded meeting him face-to-face. But he didn't show up that first weekend as planned, and by the time he left a message saying he'd be hopping by next Saturday instead, it was too late to change my tickets.

My sister wasn't at the arrivals gate as she and I had arranged. Nor was she waiting at the baggage carousel or outside in the press of the pickup zone. A wet snow, grimy even before it splatted against the windshields of the cars, partly explained her delay, so I positioned myself between one set of glass doors and another to wait. Living in Oshkosh, Wisconsin, I didn't mind the dismal rush of the real world every once in a while and resolved that my gritty perch at La Guardia was as good a place as any to indulge in it. I waited half an hour, my feet going numb in the draft from the doors, my eyebrows disheveled by gusts of wind, before pulling my bag to a cluster of phones. My fingers were so cold I dropped the quarters three times before pushing them into the slot. Then I pressed my ear to the busy signal for longer than necessary, hoping Soonie might get the vibes of her sister standing there.

Finally I phoned an operator and was told Soonie's line was off the hook. I allowed myself only a flicker of annoyance. Soonie had sounded so close to normal when I had phoned to discuss my visit that I had nearly called off the whole supposed emergency. But something had stopped me from canceling, nothing big, just a couple of offbeat moments that now that I was stranded at La Guardia seemed weirder than they had before. Like when I asked how work was going (a paralegal, Soonie worked for a publishing firm in their legal division), she answered that she didn't know which shoes she was supposed to wear anymore. And when I asked if she still attended the gym she sometimes took me to, she at once said simply, "No," offering none of her characteristically ebullient explanations.

I decided to have her paged, passed too many precious minutes listening to the blurting of the curiously Asian-sounding nickname that for long-forgotten reasons

I had given her when we were children, made a decent show of trying to decipher the public transit maps, and followed a crowd of travelers along the now-slippery sidewalk to the taxi line. I hadn't eaten in hours, so when I found an open pack of Mentos in the back of the cab, I peeled away the top few, gulped the rest, and rather than litter, slipped the grungy, fuzzy ones into my purse.

Soonie lived on Riverside Drive, but the coincidence of the names of our two patches of geography only made their differences more apparent. Compared to Soonie's genuine waterway, my Fox River at home in Wisconsin resembled a strip of foil meant to be a river seen through a miniature window in one of Leo's set-design models. When I was home I never doubted my fondness for my scrappy excuse for a town, where a bakery sign recently bravely proclaimed: NEW! TRY IT! HARD-CRUSTED BREAD! and where one of my favorite Veterans Day pastimes was driving to the Saxeville cemetery to watch the cows munching the tiny American flags. But here in New York City I couldn't help but imagine that I had made a terrible mistake in living so far from my sister, who was too innocent, I felt, to be left to herself in the noise of the city, just as I was too sharp to make do with the soft, milky heart of Wisconsin. Soonie and I should be living close by, able to watch out for each other.

Outside my sister's building sat two giant square urns for the planting of flowers, and when the cab drove away and I was climbing the slushy steps, my head averted from the slapping clumps of snow, I saw that Soonie was there in wet lamplight, emptying a giant bag of shrimp into one of them.

On top of the shrimp she emptied a carton of frozen scallops, and even as I said her name and asked what on earth she was doing, she tore open a package of crab legs and starting laying them out by the handful, her fingers purple with frost, the air smelling of seaweed. She was wearing the fake Mongolian lamb's-wool coat we had bought her on sale on my most recent visit (Labor Day) and with which she had been so pleased she wore it home from the store in eighty-degree weather, earning stares of approval along the way. She was more delicately built than I, less sarcastic looking, and much prettier. The coat would have been tawdry on me but on Soonie it was funky and adorable.

Tonight the coat had been turned inside out, to protect it from the weather, I guessed, except that the lining of lilac-colored satin was now a ruined mess of water stains and running, oozing dye. A shrimp was caught in her hair, and when I reached to dislodge it, she stood as still as the lampposts, blinking at me.

"This will keep the seafood fresh. The pork and chicken are over there. Do you think I bought enough watercress, Jaynee? Jacob told me I did but then he got out from under my feet, thank God. He even took his music. If they're not going to help us they can at least let us do our things in peace."

Jacob was her current J (since all Soonie's men turned out to have names that started with J, that was the word we used for boyfriends), whom I had never met. His photo reminded me a little of Leo, and though I hoped for her sake he was gone for good, I was furious with him for leaving Soonie to herself at a time like this.

THE BELL AT THE END OF A ROPE

Leaving the mountains of meats and seafood behind, I led my sister upstairs to her apartment, where she right-sideouted the smeary, matted coat and hung it meticulously on a coat stand. The apartment was laid out railroad-style, and as we passed from room to room, heading for the kitchen, I noticed nothing new but a couple of posters—a piglet in a picnic basket, a kitten snuggling with a basket of thong panties—added to her usual sentimental collection.

Still, the closer we came to the kitchen the more I dreaded what I would find, and even dreading it, I needed to stop short in the doorway. Arrayed all around were the rest of the ingredients for the same delicious meal—a Chinese New Year Fire Pot—that Soonie "cooked" for me whenever I came to visit, except that usually we hit the shops together and bought the wontons and noodles already fried, the sauces prepared. The modest helpings of seafood and chicken would then be cooked at the table in a fondue pot, the torn greens and the peanuts and chopsticks arranged on a single ceremonial platter. But this time she had bought the ingredients herself, as if to prepare the feast from scratch, and from the look of things there was enough to make a meal for forty or fifty people, the stubby countertop so crammed with cans of hot bean paste and bottles of rice wine and sesame oil that the packages of noodles had needed to be stacked on the floor.

"Don't tell me we're entertaining the entire NBA again," I joked, because I wanted to be missing something, wanted to give Soonie the benefit of the doubt, wanted to *be* in doubt, wanted to be persuaded that my shock and dismay were nothing but a small-towner's overreaction to the usual frayed edges of urban sanity.

Soonie stopped tapping her foot long enough to give a modest shrug of her shoulders. The gesture soothed me but only because I recognized it—it was the same shrug I made if I was embarrassed.

"Well . . . but I don't know if she'll come," Soonie shyly divulged, and started combing her damp, tangled hair with her fingers.

I peeked into the refrigerator, which wasn't properly closed, owing to all the cabbage and watercress in it. A single wok, empty, emanated a nearly molten warmth from where it balanced on the stove. I stepped forward to shut off the flame. My sister had written to Geraldine Ferraro, it turned out, inviting her for supper as a show of support over Ferraro's loss of the vice presidency ages and ages ago. Soonie showed me the invitation she had made for the ex-congresswoman, a perfectly suitable invitation if you were inviting the usual social acquaintances. The handwriting was recognizably Soonie's— no loopiness or crazed, zany slants, a hand as stable and as grounded as my own—but the dinner party was to have started an hour ago.

"So this is Geraldine Ferraro's invitation," I said evenly.

"Yeah," said Soonie.

"So it isn't a copy."

"No," said Soonie.

"So it looks like you neglected the small requirement of mailing it," I continued in good humor, still determined to speak to my sister as if she were her normal self making the kinds of mistakes that even ordinarily competent people, like Soonie, sometimes make. Or maybe this was some kind of kid-sister thing, Soonie testing me to see how unimaginative I had become out there in the Dairy State, where if you asked for imported fromage, they offered you Swiss.

"So," I added, playing for sanity the way some people play for time, "I was worried when you didn't show up at the airport, you know. I thought maybe something had happened. Mom and Dad say you seem out of sorts, these days."

"Mom and Dad," she sighed, rolling her eyes like we always did. "Well it turns out I don't have my car. Sorry, Jaynee. I gave it away."

Not too much later, we made a show of going to bed, Soonie in her bedroom and I on the foldout couch within sight of the cat climbing the pyramids of cans on the dark kitchen counter. When I closed my eyes it was to listen to my sister pacing the floor, and when I opened them again it was to find her standing over me, twisting off ends of her hair. Of all that had gone on that day so far, this mute attack on her treasured hair was the most disturbing—the way it dropped to the floor in little pinched-off black fringes resembling the odd hieroglyphics she finally typed on her laptop for me to gape at. They looked like this:

✻≈H✦   H✦   ◆≈♍   ▢■●⌂   ✦☾⌂   ◆♍ ♏☾■   ◆☾●&

What it said was, *This is the only way we can talk*, although I didn't know this until Soonie had shown me how to make the translation, the merest click of the mouse turning the symbols into the apparently passé Roman alphabet and then, *click*, into the funny symbols again. How whimsical they looked, but my courage gave way to a tremulous dread as soon as her meaning crept into me.

"*What* is the only way we can talk?" I pleaded, giving a little jump when she snatched back the laptop in her direction.

✶✵⌘✵⌘✦, she urgently typed. Then she sat bolt upright, gazed a moment at the word, and as if throwing darts, punched in three eager ✏✏✏'s beside it.

"You want us to talk like *this*?" I asked, and gestured at the pencil-shaped exclamation marks, bracing myself for the vigorous *yes* she would nod in reply. *It has to be private*, she wrote. For a moment I believed that all our troubles might be solved if only computers had never been invented. When that sorry thought fizzled I hoped maybe a cup of warm milk might do it.

✋ ✦✵✦ ✋ ✵◻✦⌘ ✦●♏♏◻, Soonie wrote.

I wish I could sleep, my click of the button translated.

✶✵♏■ ⌘✵⌘ ◻◻✦ ✵✵✦♏ ✺✦✺◻ ◻◻✦◻ ♏✺◻◻✐, I asked her. Which was, *When did you give away your car?* Except by mistake I typed *car* as *cat*, causing Soonie to panic, thinking maybe she had.

Soonie answered that she hadn't slept in nine nights, and that she'd given away the Mitsubishi on Wednesday. She explained this to me with her signature patience, the same crease forming between her eyes as when we were little girls doing homework. Her lashes were sloppy with rained-on mascara, and the bruised spots she made when she squeezed at the crease were almost as bad as the pinched-off hair.

Even so, hours later, as we conferred in the corridor of the hospital psych ward, the most her doctor would tell me was that we needed to observe my sister as carefully as possible in order to make sense of what might be going on in her head. "We'll know more when the meds kick in again," was as much as he would offer.

"What meds? Again? Soonie's on meds? How long has this been going on?" I asked, feeling a thunk of utter heartbrokenness. As girls, Soonie and I had been so in synch with each other that when we brushed each other's hair, it was nearly impossible to tell who was brushing whose. Even during our twenties, me clinging to marriage with Leo and Soonie to marriage with John the Second, we had struggled together with trying to have babies—that bevy of noisy, long-haired cousins that never came into being. And though in recent years I'd found myself taking longer than before to turn the corners of my sister's mind, I'd understood this to be the result of the vast half continent we'd plunked between us.

"Maybe she didn't want to upset *you*," the doctor answered in his disarming way of emphasizing select words. He wore Birkenstock sandals, and somehow at the sight of his damp woolen socks I understood the news that he was trying not to break to me. The reason he wasn't telling me much was that he was forbidden. Confidentiality and all that. I imagined the furrow deepening in Soonie's brow when he had asked her if I was someone in whom he might confide, the way she bowed her oval head in contemplation, the straightness of her part, its faintest quiver when she shook her head no.

"Don't worry," the doctor offered feebly. "She'll be better in a matter of days."

"Better medicated, you mean. She'll still be sick," I argued.

"In a way," he conceded. "But that's like saying that *the only reason we're not starving is that we are eating.*"

"Or that *the only reason we're not naked is that we are wearing clothes,*" I said to him, watching him slide a pen into the top of his clipboard. What I had earlier mistaken for dandruff in his hair was turning out to be flakes of melting snow. Outside the windows the snow was still falling, and the hallways were spotted with footprints that faded with time, like the smudged tracks of souls departing their bodies.

When the doctor turned to go, I didn't try to stop him, only watched him walk away in his appealingly down-to-earth costume. He'd told me nothing of Soonie's condition, but what this really boiled down to was that I was rescued from having anything substantial to tell our parents. I pictured them cooking their daily oatmeal, my father measuring water into the bowls, my mother carefully setting the microwave, their shared cholesterol level lower than a Japanese newborn's. I pictured them pumping their bicycle tires and pedaling side by side to work until my father turned left and my mother turned right, and then arriving home that evening ten minutes apart, both of them having stopped at separate video stores and rented the same movie, which they would put off watching anyway, in favor of playing Ping-Pong. Part of me dreaded having to listen to them ask each other what both of their daughters could be so "anxious" about, while another part of me didn't want to have to make them believe me just yet. I couldn't bear the idea of their flying out here to witness the awful truth for themselves and then pretend that everything was fine. How serene they always were, sending Soonie and me into fits of laughter. Heads could drop around them, bombs go off, whole countries slide off into the ocean, and our parents would just keep reading the newspaper, passing each day's news between them as amicably as if it were one of their neatly sliced pears.

There was yet another reason I didn't want to call our parents, I realized as I snuck past Soonie's troubled-sounding snores on my way to have a shower in her hospital bathroom, and that was that if I told them what was happening, then I would also need to tell them why I knew so little about it. I couldn't stand for them to know that Soonie had rejected me the way she apparently had. I was too proud. Besides, they depended on us sisters to be confidants—the pretty one (Soonie) and the maybe not entirely horsey-looking one (me). They relied on us taking care of each other, and we relied on it too, faced with our parents' unflappable pair-dom, or *pear-dom* as we called it.

Then, in the oddly triangular shower stall, which sported a variety of faucets and handrails but no effective way of adjusting the aim of the nozzle, it occurred to me that maybe our parents knew. Maybe they were the ones she had told the doctor it was okay to tell. I squeezed too hard on the soap, thinking of this. It flew out of my hand, shot over the top of the shower stall, and landed nowhere that I could find. Maybe our parents were flying in at this moment, dressed in the matching tops they reserved for airplane travel, sweatshirts with an old Dewey decimal system catalog card for a volume of Victorian love letters silk-screened on them.

I decided that if they did finally show up, I would say my hellos and good-byes and go back to Wisconsin in time to lead the DNR man through his condominium, pointing out the grounded outlets where he could safely plug in the power-surge protectors he needed for the hatching lights on his terrariums.

In the visitor's chair near Soonie's hospital bed, I dreamed of newts, salamanders, and toads, and of fucking the biologist on the carpeted floor of the bedroom loft before his mattresses arrived. This worried me a little, because I really couldn't stand the sound of his voice. Besides, Soonie never used any form of "to fuck." Instead she used variants of "to be intimate with," her compromise between screwing around and falling in love. I had something to learn from Soonie, I realized, like not viewing sex as a method of conquest even when we were partying, making all sorts of men go goggle-eyed. And she had things to learn from me, like not succumbing to what I couldn't help but think of as a frivolous temptation to do and say whatever insane thing popped into her head. Of course I was ashamed of my intolerance. Soonie wasn't being frivolous, she was only being mentally ill. But I found this idea even harder to bear. And when I woke again much later in the darkened room, it was to find one of the psych-ward patients crouching over me.

For a moment I thought the figure was Soonie's. She must have wakened from her rest, must have tried, at least, to improve on the job she had started on her hair, for it had traded its pinched-off ends for an outdated puffed-up flip that reminded me of the set of molded-plastic toy wigs, like translucent helmets, that she and I had dressed up in as little girls.

I pulled myself up in my chair, was offered a cup of cold 7UP with the straw bent just so, and saw that Soonie's bed was empty, the sheets drawn smooth.

"Pretend you're a believer," this odd figure encouraged.

I clasped my hands as if in prayer, like in the hospital logo.

"Now pretend you are describing God to me. What would you say?"

Across the hall in the patient lounge, a man was crawling in circles around the magazine table, as he'd been doing the whole time I'd been there. Who were these poor unfortunates, I wanted to know. What tidings did they bring? I felt both sorry for and weary of my untoward visitor, her silly lace collar, her melancholy eyes, the hairdo that even *I* knew wasn't retro but simply old-fashioned, and I wondered about all the possible circumstances that might have landed her in this H-shaped configuration of hallways, with its air of a retreat, minus the relaxation. The person before me looked restful enough but as if, if I said the wrong thing, she might drop with a clatter. Even so I let my finger hover above the nurse call button, like a teller too captivated by the bank robber to set off the alarm.

What could I possibly say about God, I wondered? How would I describe Him, or Her, or It, or Them? Soonie and I were atheists. We couldn't help it, we'd been brought up that way. Our parents were both lapsed Jews, and this casual fact bore no more conviction than if they'd laid a sandwich on a plate and neglected to eat it. Sometimes we wished we had something bigger than us to believe in, something stronger than everything else and that distinguished itself from love, sex, and money by taking at least a couple of seconds to gaze on the messes it brought into being.

"God's the J I'll never meet," I decided, opting for the metaphor instead of the demurral. "God's the J out there someplace our paths won't cross, where He can disregard me even though He doesn't know I exist. For the record, this isn't a bad thing. His and my relationship can't get screwed up, I mean."

"No, it can't," the psych patient agreed, gathering up my cup and straw. When she was gone and I opened my hands, half expecting to find something left in them— a loose screw, maybe—there was only the lemony scent of her gloominess. I thought it perversely delightful, compared to the nurses' cheerful greetings.

Later that day I phoned my answering machine at Riverside Condos, found a rubbery message from the Department of Natural Resources man telling me that he would be another week late moving in, then emailed my boss, pretending to be in my office. After that I bided my time, cleaning shrimp from the urns at Soonie's apartment building and passing whole chunks of time with her at the hospital, taking long, damp walks to get from one to the other while fiddling for those grungy Mentos at the bottom of my purse, not to eat them of course but just to know I didn't have to. Generally, I avoided Soonie's doctor, or maybe he avoided me. In any case, the doctors stopped by the hospital only briefly each morning, reminding me of the adage An Apple a Day Keeps the Doctor Away, except that they seemed to have twisted it up somehow in their favor. Soonie appeared to be getting neither better nor worse, or rather, to be doing both things at once. No matter how optimistic I felt each time I approached the hospital—

imagining us once again chatty and girlish, she at the head of the bed and me at the foot, our shoes askew on the floor, our legs crossed one on top of the other as she told me about the group therapy sessions in a dazed but philosophical tone—I would be disappointed to find her hunched over a drawing pad, working up psychedelic publicity for a book she was calling *The Geraldine Ferraro on the Go Salad Cookbook*. Every so often she paused at her drawing, her feet too far apart, her beautiful, compact, sensual body a perplexed, disjointed question mark, and then we might glance at each other with crushed expressions, both of us knowing how lonely the other one felt but being unable to join her and comfort her.

But in less clumsy moments we found ourselves poised to regard her illness as if it had been the result of some accident or other—"a fall down the steps of my mind," explained Soonie—from which she was in the process of making a recovery. She allowed me to phone the upstairs neighbor to get back her car, and we straightened the pinched-off ends of her hair with some scissors I snuck in from home. On her laptop she proposed to me in Wingdings that we swear off our excesses. Not even the most appropriate, toothbrush-toting J would be welcome at Soonie's, and the string of casual bedfellows waiting for me in Wisconsin would be told off promptly when I returned. We would be celibate, Soonie declared, and when I asked what the doctor thought of this notion, she replied it was none of his business what women did with their bodies.

One morning, I was informed that the hospital social worker was hoping to meet with me. I rode the elevator down to the lobby, turned past the ugly fountain where people tossed pennies, stalled at the entrance to the cafeteria, considering a hot cocoa detour, and finally knocked on the office door. I can't say I was entirely surprised to find that same wigged-out patient, the one who had asked me to describe God, motioning me to a chair, a lacquered wooden chair with a smaller butt than mine carved into it. Her old-fashioned dress was similar to the one she had worn before, only this one had an elastic empire waist, which to my eye makes people look like drawstring sacks in which they are lugging around their own body parts. Today an ID tag—Sister B. Potts, Social Worker—was pinned to the neckline, and hanging on the wall I saw a framed needlepoint with the same title done up in stitches. Beyond a window lay a courtyard under snow, some stiff grass poking through, and a concrete bench with a single bottom's worth of snow swept off for sitting. Days pass differently in hospitals than anywhere else. Whole lives begin here while others expire, and meanwhile we visitors are pedaling air.

"As long as you've made your way down here," she invited, "I'd like to ask you how you and your sister are doing. You know, if there's anything new you'd like to talk about, Jaynee. Or old, maybe. I'm just trying to help. I'm just trying to get to the bottom of things."

Of course I didn't tell her that I had once mistaken her for a patient, mainly because I figured she already knew. She was one of those dead-smart people. It would have been scary to be regarded by her if her gaze were not so liquid, so forgiving. She seemed to be looking right through me to what I was grappling with—my sad side thinking how awful it was for my sister to be sick, and my uppity side thinking what a cop-out it was for Soonie to come so unglued, what a play for attention, what a good-for-nothing way of overcoming life's daily obstacles it was to crawl around a coffee table or paste rickrack on an oven mitt along with a roomful of other dropouts from society.

But Sister Potts's brown eyes were like certain places—the bathtub, your own kitchen late at night—where you could simply be yourself without doubt or uncertainty. She didn't even appear to be wearing a bra, though when I went braless it was for very much the opposite of the earthy effect B. Potts projected. Soonie too. Even when we were teenagers, our parents had excused our wayward dress as being a less self-destructive method of rebellion than what other kids were doing. Braless was better than topless, marijuana was better than heroin, promiscuity was better than getting paid for it, and so on. What was psychosis better than, I wondered? They—our parents—appeared to be the real thing Sister Potts hoped to talk about. Should we give them a call? Were they coming or weren't they? Why should I continue to go out of my way to preserve our parents' incomparable, unruffled bliss? Shouldn't they get their faces rubbed in the opposite of ignorance, just like I was?

"What have you told them?" Sister Potts asked.

"I told them everything was basically going okay, but that was a while ago," I admitted.

"So all you'd need to do is tell them now it's not," Sister Potts reasoned, pushing the phone gently toward me across the desktop. "The doctors won't have called them, that's for sure. And who can blame Soonie for not telling them herself? If I were hallucinating, I wouldn't want to be the one to tell my parents about it, either."

"My sister's not hallucinating!" I argued.

"Delusions are a variant. I'm sorry, Jaynee. Has there ever been anything like this in the rest of your family? And did you ever witness your sister having delusions or anything before a couple of years ago, maybe back when you were children? There might have been something she did, or felt, something that—"

"Not unless thinking life is worth living *anyway* is a delusion," I answered with certainty.

Sister Potts grimaced, as if she really did believe that thinking life worth living might be a delusion, and though under other circumstances I might have pressed her on this issue, I understood that such an inquiry might lead us to the subject of God again, within sight of Sister Potts's bench in the snowy courtyard with its altar of chimney and mourning dove, its arched ceiling of sky.

"As for calling our parents," I began . . . but then I paused in thought, trying to figure out how best to explain my reluctance to phone them. I told her that on their frequent trips to wilderness areas, they often asked other sightseers to snap their photo. The most recent of these photos showed them facing away from the camera, gazing out at a plume of black smoke from an actual forest fire, their floppy sunhats unruffled, their rear trouser pockets bulging with maps and bottled water.

"That's my parents," I said. "Watching stuff burn up, then heading back where they came from for lunch and a nap. They even talk alike. They have similar voices, I mean," I said, letting my own voice drop to their shared, velvety register, the sound of which shocked me for how unexpectedly it caused me to miss them.

"Looks to me like maybe they're just standing tall, you know, like some of us do, trying to be sturdy and reliable and brave and maybe even protect you," Sister Potts suggested.

I said I'd never thought of them that way. I told her that Soonie and I used to be jealous of people whose parents fought and argued, people whose mothers sat around in bathrobes smoking cigarettes all morning and whose dads got drunk at night. I said our parents had loved and respected us, clothed, fed, talked to, admired, and cared for us. Then I raised my hands above my head, bared my teeth at poor Sister Potts and shouted, "Attack of nerves! Attack of nerves! Attack of nerves! Attack of nerves!"

She only sat gazing at me, her eyes unblinking but struck through with layers of rich gold color, like tiger's-eye stones.

" 'Attack of nerves' is what our parents said when they called me and asked me to come here," I explained. "They said it would be good for me to get a break from work and do my hair with Soonie."

"Yes, but if they hadn't called, you wouldn't have known how much she needed you," Sister Potts reminded me. "Just like if you don't call them, they won't know she needs them, either."

It was then that there came a knock at the office door and in walked a man pulling a flat, wheeled cart. He parked the dolly behind where I sat, handed a folded note to Sister Potts, and went to stand in the hallway. Sister Potts laid the note on the blotter unread and asked if I might help her load up her belongings. She looked beaten, suddenly. I could tell she had both dreaded and reconciled herself to this eventuality, as if she really were one of the patients, and the real Sister Potts had been locked in the closet, and it was only a matter of time before the mix-up was discovered. But in the closet stood only an empty paper towel box, so we passed a few minutes emptying her desk drawers into it and pulling a few pictures, along with the needlepoint, off the walls. Next went a handful of books, a nubbly cardigan sweater, and a single coffee mug with an outdated version of the hospital logo on it. *"The reason we're here is that we're not somewhere else,"* I said to her, perturbed by how little there was of this office, how meager the depths underneath its spare surface. The man wheeled the loaded dolly into the hallway, leaving behind some accordion files bursting with papers, and two empty clothes hangers. As he aimed the cart for the loading dock, there was something about the droop of Sister Potts's hemline that made me see the significance of what had just occurred. Her whole life revolved around that humdrum, dismal little office, and in just under thirteen minutes it had been packed up, wheeled up the ramp to the parking lot, and parked under a tree from which dangled a sorry-looking string of forgotten Christmas bulbs.

"What's going on?" I let myself ask as together we maneuvered it to her car. I helped her load the trunk, which wouldn't close properly over the paper towel box. Seeing no rope to tie it with, I fetched the Christmas lights instead, the bulbs trailing on the pavement after I yanked on the knot.

"Because I talk too much," Sister Potts answered evenly. "Doctors like to be the only ones that know things. For instance, they believe that informed patients will take on the symptoms expected of them. Like if you tell a patient he's self-destructive, he'll start hoarding razors," she explained, adding what a shame it was the theory didn't work in the opposite direction, "like if you tell the doctor he runs the risk of not being a jerk, he might start giving a shit about other people. And also because I show poor judgment, like would you like a ride home?"

Despite her vehemence she drove with some hesitancy, causing minor jams and gridlocks at the merest sight of a pedestrian crosswalk, but then taking the turns so close to the curbs we could have plucked the wallets out of people's back pockets.

As it happened, I could have used the money. When Sister Potts had dropped me off at Soonie's apartment, I found a message to call my boss in Wisconsin. The DNR man wasn't coming, it turned out, and a shipment of toads that he must have arranged to have delivered to my office had died in their Styrofoam cooler while waiting for me to mail them back. Meanwhile, a deer had died on the condominium grounds, having wandered through town and stepped off our dock onto too-thin ice. Since no one but me had the gumption to pull it up by its antlers, that was to be my last chore, after scrubbing the smell of rotted amphibian out of the mailroom and fixing the pipes I had caused to explode by neglecting to leave a trickle of water running in the DNR man's faucet during frigid weather.

OVER THE YEARS, the DNR man came to mind whenever I drove past Riverside Condos. I pictured us sharing a summery game of checkers out on the patio, our friendship testy and puritanical in deference to the pact I had made with Soonie. Men always perked up at the mention of sisters, as if one might drive up any minute and be more sympathetic toward him than the original, and in my case it would be true, I would tell him, Soonie was kinder than I was. The biologist and I would crack open a beer, stack our checker pieces in lopsided towers, and talk about whether or not it was delusional to think life was worth living, and about why we were here rather than elsewhere, and why we were clothed rather than naked, and why we ate rather than starved, and if the answers might be the same for amphibians as for human beings.

This fantasy carried a wistful air, for two reasons.

One, because of course I was getting laid all the time, my half of the vow of chastity being only a thrumming daze that came over me whenever I found myself needing to lie about it to Soonie. And two, because I wished I had kept track of Sister B. Potts, Social Worker. I wished I knew where she was and what she was doing, and if she still wore her hair in that outmoded flip. Recalling the warm, moist brown of Sister Potts's eyes, I recently asked Soonie if she had received any news of her whereabouts.

It was a dumb thing to ask. My sister always becomes abstracted when I refer to her stay in the hospital, as if she thinks she's covering up for something. Plus, at the time, we were at our parents' house, which is always kind of an eye-rolling place for us to be. She and I had met at Detroit Metro airport and flown together to Indianapolis. In Detroit we had lost each other in terminal A, paged each other, found each other in terminal C, lost each other again in one or another restroom, and finally been stuck on the runway for two hours and twenty-five minutes, me fiddling with those Mentos still in my purse, the two of us sharing an Einstein Bagels' Veggie Schmear sandwich. Now it was way past midnight, our parents safely in bed, and we were ironing the clothes we would wear the next day for our parents' fiftieth-anniversary party. Their house was all in twos—two reading chairs, two plates in the dish rack, two library books (both about global warming) on the coffee table, but there was only one iron. We were steeling ourselves against the morning, knowing we'd be faced with Jimmy and Judy Horvathe, Gail and Peter Schuller, Dick and Joany Minch, and the rest of our parents' numerous friends whose names came in pairs, or pears, we said.

I have never been good at ironing. In my hands, ironing is more like pleating, and then like more and more pleating, trying to get the first pleat out. I smoothed in another mistaken pleat, and asked Soonie if she thought she might ever tell our parents about her illness.

"Should I?" she asked with a tilt of her head, a little sympathetic nudge at the air in my direction.

I put down the iron but kept clear of my glass of wine, a slender, lone stem because Soonie wasn't supposed to drink alcohol. I thought of what Sister B. Potts had said to me, about some people standing tall, trying to be reliable and sturdy and brave, even when they were most afraid. It wasn't like I remembered this idea from out of nowhere, standing in our parents' kitchen. Rather, I remember it always. It's part of me, like my long hair. I wear it up, I wear it down, I brush it, Soonie brushes it, I wear it twisted, I wear it hidden—it's always the same shape-shifting thing.

"I don't know," I answered truthfully. "But do you ever wonder what happened to the social worker?"

"Oh, her! She married the doctor!" Soonie happily exclaimed, and made a move for the wine, our fingers meeting at the stem, the glass remaining somehow upright between us. "The doctor with the Birkenstocks! The doctor who refused to tell me anything about you and all that you were going through, poor sweet you. Can you believe that, Jaynee?"

No. I can't.

Not a chance, I tell myself.

Except I see the words like this: ☠□♦ ♋ ♍♒♋■♍♏✐✐✐ and have to study them a moment, really ponder those three exclamatory pencils, before I look away.

BROKEN MAP

THE MAN WHO CATCHES MY EYE or, let's face it, does not, from where he jogs around the track, is . . . what . . . a thoracic surgeon? I discern, in the crags of his enthusiastic face: all the years and years at Harvard Medical School; the stolen minutes of unconsciousness on a cot in a physicians' locker room; the daily exchanging of scrubs for workout gear; the kindly scientific eyes; a fond, efficient, apologetic smile. Also some knowledge of what a thorax is and where it lives in the body. And like whether a person might die of one or not, and what one feels like in the hand. His eyes: green and amused. In the bathroom of his penthouse (this too I can see in the crags of his face), he tends two daddy longlegs, pets, which inhabit a corner high over the tub. He keeps the windows wide open so they can catch gnats. He is careful where he steps, careful to close the toilet seat. When by mistake he nearly crushes one of his spiders, he lays it on its back on a square of toilet paper, and with a pencil and surgical tweezers, he uncurls its scrunched legs and places it safe on its towel rod to "heal thyself." Because it's tough to spin webs on porcelain tile, he lets them borrow the corners of towels.

Later I spot the kindly surgeon sudsing up a busted car on one of the postage-stamp lawns on Smith Street. Smith Street is more the idea of a street than an actual street. Picture the globe scattered here and there with shoebox-like houses, and God remarking, "It would be good for them to devise a system of narrow corridors for getting from one little dwelling to another via automobile."

But there's a kid chasing after a basketball today on Smith Street, and even a gas station selling lottery tickets at the Jackson Road intersection. I'm driving my boy, Thomas, to high school. In our kitchen this morning, rather than finishing his breakfast of blueberries and toast, he sat sketching a preliminary portrait of Prime Minister Patrick Manning, of Trinidad and Tobago. He likes to sketch them all twice. Having done the dimpled cheeks, he paused for a moment before shading the cleft of the chin, his upraised fingers making incremental shading marks in air. Jumped three grades by a string of baffled teachers, he's youngest in his class by nearly four years. A few of the girls are smaller than he, as is one of the teachers (music), but none of the boys. At lunch he sits with kids who drill him on zip codes of capital cities and how to say swear words in foreign languages. He finds the faces online—for every week, a new prime minister—and hangs his sketches on a map he adds to with newspaper articles, and he tapes all this on the wall of my bedroom, since the wall in his bedroom is way too small. He has knobby knuckles, colored pencils. I worry kids laugh at his cool tinted Prime Minister Nuri Kamal al-Maliki–style eyeglasses. If I were him I would be lonesome, but he doesn't seem to be. Sometimes I ask, "Are you lonesome, Thomas?" but he only rolls his eyes. And sometimes I remark too brightly to him, "When you get married—" or "When you have children, I'll—" in order to learn if, at twelve years old, he scoffs at the likelihood of normal things ever happening to him, but he doesn't scoff, he only rolls his eyes. He's a private sort of boy. He rarely divulges. Normal in normal ways, I mean. Loved, I mean. Loving. The idea of him grown, eternally solitary, passing the right person by without the two of them knowing to stop for a moment to fall in love with each other, opens a chasm of pain in me. I'm sucked into it, I mean. And there's a song I sometimes hear on the radio, about a man who goes a hundred years without ever finding his soul mate (who is always, of course, just around the corner searching for *her* soul mate), that makes me crawl five miles on cobbles in my mind and light candles on an altar.

On Saturday mornings, when Thomas sits in my room for hours on end regarding his sketches, his map, the clefts of the chins, I imagine him, instead, playing that old-fashioned maze game—the wooden box with the heavy, silvery marble, the two sanded wooden knobs and the tilting, swiveling maze—with friends.

Outside the surgeon's house stand two ordinary wooden birdhouses and one hummingbird trumpet, which suggests to me he isn't a thoracic specialist, really, at all, but an ornithologist supplementing his Department of Natural Resources income by marketing himself as a freelance consultant for prairie rejuvenation and wetlands preservation projects. He organizes sandhill crane counts. He oversees testing for the presence of toxins in oriole eggs. I know this isn't so. Well, if it is, I'll be shocked. I mean I know I am only imagining things, like the day I was certain that a phone call I missed was my sister calling to say that our inheritance had been miscalculated. And like when I fell in love with that soulful composer who turned out to be a severely mentally disabled person who feared deep down that he was really an onion. And like once, when my son lay asleep in his crib, I said to myself, "Get used to it," meaning, I needed to accept that he was really a creature disguised as a boy, sent from another planet in order to transmit observations about earthling moms for a celestial *Wikipedia*. I really did (do) believe these things . . . but at the same time I knew (know) that I was (am) making them up. At other times, the balance shifts: I know I make them up, but even so, I can't help but believe in them. Like he isn't divorced, the DNR ornithologist/surgeon. Instead he's widowed, still mourning. There's a daughter, fifteen. Widowed, grieving, he bought her her first box of pads, two training bras, the absolute wrong-style underpants. You can tell from her manner there on the lawn, hosing hollyhock stalks, that her patience with him is turning lately, just barely, to tolerance. From across the cafeteria she gapes at my son in the handsome Peruvian blouse I bought him, the blouse crowded with Tony Blair and Indira Gandhi buttons.

    Finally I pay a visit to two hairdressers I know who might get a thrill out of setting me up. I pull them out of their twilit firefly reverie in their garden one evening and drive them to Smith Street, where together, side by side in white trousers, they walk to the ornithologist's door. He opens it topless, backlit by greenish flickerings. He doesn't ask them in. Probably less than a minute goes by. I stay in the car in the breezy, warm dark. He disappears from the threshold, comes back holding a notebook and pen, prints out his name and number, and pulls the page from the spiral with such uncanny precision that every flake of white paper remains attached.

EVEN IF HIS NAME WEREN'T THOMAS, same as my son's, I'd have liked him right away on the telephone, especially his apology to me for not having noticed me at the YMCA, or imagined who I am or how much money do I have or did I lose, like in the stock market (fat chance), and what kinds of sorrows.

But he's out of a job, it turns out when we meet for our date a night or two later. He picks me up in his car, which is basically a muffler being dragged along on wheels. And despite the birdhouses, he knows even less about birds than I do, now that I've researched indigo buntings in hopes we'd have something (buntings) in common. He can't do calls (sweet-sweet-chew-chew-sweet-sweet), and he doesn't know nests. He has that funny way of lisping *right here* (rye cheer) but in a bitter tone of voice as if he's mocking somebody. We are seated at Fratellos with two pints of stout and a platter of nachos. I don't need to look away from him in order to relinquish the idea of his calling yellow-headed warblers to us from out of the trees, or of his holding a thorax, like a bird, in his hand . . . but nevertheless I exercise a moment of private, inner silence in order to slide these debunked fantasies into a separate, less unreasonable part of my mind. I feel a click inside, and then a gentle whirring motion as I let them slide past. I do the same for his face, of which the weather-beaten crags, now that I'm seeing them so close up, aren't rugged, exactly, but have been sanded away a grain at a time. I have no right to be disappointed in him. Not once has he pretended to be the person I'd hoped he was. I only balance a whole black olive on half a tortilla chip, and try to lift it to my mouth without knocking it off.

"What kind of job were you laid off from?" I ask.

We are seated at the bar on stools so high that when my shoe (platform) falls off my foot, it makes a dent in the platform of my other shoe, which fell off before.

"Loading dock," Tom answers. "Only I wasn't laid off, I should probably say. I was fired. Only please don't ask me why. Not a word. Okay? Never. Promish me," the funny lisp emphasized.

I still want him in bed, want it not with my legs so much anymore as with other parts of me that worry all those fireflies might have been wasted if we simply part ways. Their brief hour on earth wasted. By me, I mean. No lovers watching them blink on and off in the garden, I mean, as a result of my leading the two hairdressers away from their reverie of them. Fireflies survive for but three or four evenings. Basically they screw, reproduce, and die. I guess we'll smoke a cigarette after our dinner, Tom and me. I picture him ferrying crates of cigarette cartons up the loading ramp at Kmart, along those spinning metal tubes. I picture us lounging side by side smoking, even though we both quit a long time ago, in order to enjoy doing the thing we most enjoy doing, at least once, together. People with money, like in the stock market, don't understand the value of a pleasure like smoking, which compared to other pleasures costs practically nothing, moneywise, which especially since the inheritance really did turn out to have been miscalculated is something I need to keep in mind. You need to factor in all sorts of other things too. Like all the places you'll sit when you're smoking, the benches with views designed for being looked at while smoking, the stairways and doorways within which the meanings of things are made clearer by smoking there. When I first noticed the crazy noncomposer, for instance, the one who fears he is an onion, he was sitting on just such a bench, not smoking but contemplative, self-contained, a man of thin skin but deep, spiraling layers. It's not sex I crave so much as to have certain layers deeply in common with the person I'm doing it with. The minute Tom and I light up a cigarette after our dinner, we'll have something in common because we'll be smoking. And if we sit on a bench, we'll have something else in common because we'll be sitting on the same bench.

"What's your favorite time of day for reading the newspaper?" I ask.

"Monday and Tuesday evenings." That's when he feels most alone, he adds. He gives a fond, efficient, apologetic smile, just like the smile I had imagined.

"And why do you feel most alone on Monday and Tuesday evenings?" My bare foot thumps against a chair leg. The other practices its arch: point, flex, point, rotate, cramp. I've already warned him I'll ask what I wish. It's up to him whether he answers or not.

Because that's when his daughter, who has field hockey, prayer group, and band practice on other nights, is most likely to be holed up in her room, postponing a game of Parcheesi with him.

"You play board games?" I ask. "So do I!"

THE FIRST THING HE DOES when we get to his house is introduce me to his dog, whose name is Sushi, and then he shows me the basement that he hadn't quite finished refinishing when he ran out of what he calls "funds."

The rooms have space at the top for a new false ceiling. The ceiling grid has been hung, but the stacks of new tiles will be returned to Home Depot as soon as he finds the sales receipt, which is in his lost wallet, which is why I paid for the nachos and stout. In the space above the walls, which are of the same consistency as Rice Krispies bars and which you can practically push right over just by not even really leaning on them, can be seen some pipes and coils amid cobwebs and bare bulbs that make me wonder if the spiders have enough to eat up there.

I ask Tom what he thinks might be appropriate names for the spiders, assuming that they are mother and son. So we stand side by side in the unfinished basement thinking up names. Maude and Timothy. Penny and Dime. Beyond the grid for the nonexistent ceiling can be seen the glowing margins of another zone, to which Sushi leads the way by slinking through the furnace room. Tom says that the dog makes him feel less alone on Saturdays. He follows her into a doorway with no door, and beckons me through. There's a creek in there. A heron stands on one leg in the shallows and a red-belted kingfisher perches on a branch jutting out of a log. Moss grows on the banks. There's a feeling of peace, like when you're walking at twilight, peace you know isn't real. We sit there not smoking, drinking it in. It seems churlish to smoke even imaginary cigarettes near imaginary wildlife. Our grandchildren, Tom muses—meaning not the grandchildren we might someday have together, of course, he tells me, embarrassed, but the ones that are born to our daughter and son, not that they'll have children together, either, I mean, he tells me, embarrassed—our grandchildren might be born into a world where there is no longer wildlife anywhere. Children will need to be shown pictures of indigo buntings in books in order to understand what kinds of animals birds once were. There will be videos in tiny damp rooms in museums, showing starlings in trees, and people old enough to have once seen trees will describe how much they miss them and how they pray they might someday see one again. A book of drawings of birds by a painter, Goodday or someone, sold at auction for $1.76 million some weeks ago in Paris, I say to Tom.

The heron stands still, but the kingfisher dives. Soon we step into the water ourselves, splashing and playing, but when we climb out, we're dry. You would think that he has never had a blow job before in his life for the sounds he makes, a string of whip-poor-willish cries mixed in with pleadings with me never to stop what I'm doing, never to go away, never to leave him alone. He seems truly afraid, terrified, really, that I might just stand up and walk out on him lying there. His pants are down around his ankles, his musty sneakers still tied, his knees bare where I shudder between them. I wear nothing but my camisole. When we're done, we say, "Wine."

We go back past the flimsy, unfinished walls, upstairs to the living room, to drink Sutter Creek wine out of coffee mugs at a TV table. The front door Tom opened on the night the two hairdressers alerted him to there being a person (me) interested (no longer) in possibly sharing a corner of the planet with him, is not four feet away from where we sit. The whole house is like that. Walking into it is like turning the knob on a toaster oven. Sushi pants by the door, waiting to be let out.

"So why *were* you fired?" I finally ask.

IN MID-NOVEMBER, I run into Tom again, in the waiting room at the eye-doctor clinic, where my son is inside being treated for pinkeye. There are three rows of chairs and a coffee pot. Tom offers me coffee. He drove his mother here, he tells me, and he's been waiting forty minutes to take her home. She has macular degeneration, and yes, he found his wallet. Then he gestures out the window at a sagging yellow car, and tells me he's no longer unemployed.

"Well, I should say that I'm renting, really, the car, I mean. Renting to buy. And that my new job is taking care of my mom. In her house. I had to sell mine. She pays me with social security."

He bends over to pick up my pocketbook, which has rolled off my lap. You aren't allowed to rub them—your eyes when you have pinkeye, which I've caught from poor Thomas, whose eyes are pinker than mine, itchier even than mine, more worthy of the cost of a trip to the doctor than mine, and which can be treated with hot, moist cloths, which is probably how I caught it, treating Thomas's pinkeye myself with washcloths, so as not to have to schedule this doctor visit. Because of something careless I said to him one night while we sat gazing at some lights we'd strung over his map, my son no longer sketches prime ministers.

"Thomas?" I'd said.

The lights we'd strung over the map were plastic banana pepper lights, but they were disappointingly all-American looking, like hot-dog lights or corn-on-the-cob lights would be. Funny how you say things without giving a thought as to how deeply you might someday regret having said them. Or even the same day, rue them. Or the same minute.

"I don't know that all these prime ministers deserve to have the same amount of attention given them," I said to my son. "I hate to see you lavishing so much care and so much time and all those expensive colored pencils on all of them, when some of them deserve it but some of them don't. I mean Disraeli, like you say, he passed the Climbing Boys Act, and he rebuilt the slums. And he loved novels. It must have been horrible being a chimney sweep when he was a boy. Sometimes he thought he might die up there! And he was always so cold. But William Pitt the Younger? Maybe his portrait should be smaller than Disraeli's or not so many colors."

My son did not roll his eyes. I could see the strings of banana peppers distorted in the curves of his eyeglasses, and I could tell he wasn't letting himself blink, as if he were waging a staring contest with Palestinian prime minister Ismail Haniyeh. It was clear to me, at once, that he'd made some of them up. Some of the countries on his map, I mean; I didn't know what they were. And on some of the faces, I'd never even seen eyebrows like that before, and some names of the rivers I'd never heard of before. It didn't matter to him that some of his countries were actual while some weren't, or that some of his prime ministers were good-hearted while some weren't. He believed in them, that's all. He believed in their wattles, their brows.

Sadly he pulled the map from the wall. I taped it back up. One of the corners hangs over, now. I can see it in my mind while sitting here across from Tom in the eye-doctor clinic, sipping coffee with too much creamer in it—the paper corner of the map, like a swan's wing broken there.

"But can I introduce you to my mom?" Tom asks, taking hold of my elbow and lifting me up to greet the old woman as she is led into the room. She wears giant paper sunglasses, which she is not to take off for the longest time. How frail she is. I'd forgotten she has the same name as me.

"Glad to meet you," I say, standing up to shake hands with the skinnier, more confused Annie, who seems at once to be falling to rest on me as if my body is grass for her to lie down on. "And you have such a nice son," I say to her. "You did such a good job with him!" I pause, mortified. "He's lucky to have you. You're lucky to have him too, I mean. I have a Thomas too, I mean. A son. Thomas."

"I think so too, exactly," the old woman says, sitting down on my chair. The big sunglasses slip. One eye is exposed, a desperate, blurred, hungry eye, brightly disheveled, ravenous for me.

"I'll leave you lovebirds to yourshelves, now," she lisps at us. "I won't get in your way, I promish. I'm good rye cheer."

IS GLISTENING

THROUGHOUT THE HOUSE, but mainly in the kitchen, were all sorts of objects from Mexico. The painted chair, the saltshaker in the shape of a bird, the whistle in the shape of a bird, the platter, an apron, the tablecloth. The blanket, the Oaxacan bowl, the papier-mâché skeleton, the bell on the end of a rope. And if the brooch and bracelet counted, then the brooch and bracelet, which had been made by a Norwegian living in Mexico who stamped his name—Jorgensen—into the backs, so really the jewelry counted for half. But it was made of good silver and should have cost more than it had. All the other mementos had been purchased for practically nothing on the second-to-last full day of Jenessa Saulk's parents' honeymoon, September 1, 1959.

On September 2 the newlyweds were taking a leisurely breakfast outside on the hotel terrace. Their souvenir shopping was done. The sightseeing was done and so were a couple of days at the beach with some sets of rented snorkel masks and flippers. Their clothes were nearly all packed, their tickets and passports zipped into a pouch in a hidden compartment in one of the pieces of luggage. For some time they sat dawdling over their meal while gazing down and around at the cluttered, off-season streets, wondering if they might as well pass the whole rest of their honeymoon drinking and smoking there, for it was the perfect, voluptuous day for that—the air lazy and moist, the flowers dripping like rain hats, the traffic muffled, the air blotted with cold spots like those in the ocean—when a man approached their table. His appearance was both puzzling and a relief. A relief because he wasn't a mandolin player preparing to serenade them, and puzzling because he was drinking from a yellow coffee cup like they were, even though he clearly wasn't a guest. Like a waiter, he had come from the kitchen, except he wore no vest. Instead, he wore a pressed but faded Lacoste shirt from which the crocodile appliqué had been removed, leaving behind a constellation of nearly invisible needle holes. His skin was baked brown, and his English was flawless American-style. His mustache was clipped. His name was Señor Fentin, and he was determined to take them fishing.

"How much?" asked Jenessa's dad, laying his fork onto his omelet plate to shake Fentin's well-manicured hand and await the reply.

Mr. Saulk didn't mind being interrupted while eating, but he did mind eating while he was being interrupted. He savored his food. If anyone took a taste off his plate, even Jenessa's mom, even with a clean fork like on their second date, even nothing but a parsley sprig, he wouldn't eat another bite.

Nor would he order a fresh, untouched meal. His appetite would be as if vandalized. He wouldn't be angry, only rebuked by whatever remained untouched on the plate. Tears would rise in his eyes, embarrassing him. The thing that bothered him the most if someone ate it off his plate was, oddly, the very last bite remaining, for then it would seem as if he had lingered mistakenly over something that was false—some promise that was broken.

"Twenty-five dollars US," answered Señor Fentin.

"Twenty-five dollars for both of us or each?"

For bride and groom, the man said.

A hummingbird flitted past on the terrace, looking for anything crimson to sip. Señor Fentin shooed the winged intruder away. Somehow he could tell that the Saulks were on their honeymoon. Maybe he had an eye for the groundwork being laid for a marriage, the mild flirtations and surreptitious compromises. He would sail the couple into the gulf, he averred, and, balancing his yellow cup on the railing, not on their table, presented them with a business card printed with his name and a smiling little boat. The card would be left amid the breakfast dishes there on the table, but years later, grown up, Jenessa would see in her mind that same boat tilting whimsically on waves embossed like cake icing. Even then her parents' favorite story—of the fisherman Señor Fentin and the nurse Mrs. Greene—still enjoined itself, occasionally, to reel out inside her, not in words exactly, but in a private, corporeal braille like the pinpricks left behind by the Lacoste crocodile.

"I'm not interested in paying twenty-five dollars to sit on a boat when I'm perfectly happy sitting right here," her dad had said. "What do you think, hon?" he asked his wife.

"Oh you know me," said Mrs. Saulk. "If I don't get to go fishing I kick and yell. Besides, it's chilly."

"Not on the water," said Señor Fentin. "On the water it's glistening."

"Or we can take a walk to the square instead," said Mrs. Saulk. "So, no. No thank you, Señor Fentin."

Jenessa's mom waved her coffee spoon good-bye at their personable, good-looking visitor. Then she leveled her spoon at what was left of Jenessa's dad's omelet, carved out a bite, and ate it.

"Breakfast over!" she cried.

SEÑOR FENTIN APPEARED on the square while they were taking their walk, and offered them a pair of scuffed binoculars through which to admire the view of the gulf. By aiming the binoculars along a certain sidewalk down the steepest, straightest hill, they could see some bars of sunlight combing the water under a salty, bleached-yellow sky. And from the crest of that hill they could make out Fentin's boat, smaller than a beetle but painted a vivid, piercing blue, at the end of a dock. The little child-size Mexican chair at the edge of the hearth in the Saulks' kitchen would be exactly the same shade of blue, except with lavender pansies twined around the dowels.

"I can't boat in these floppy espadrilles," Jenessa's mom said, raising the binoculars past the dock into the glare. "And I'll need a better hat."

As Señor Fentin led them on a shortcut back to the hotel, he explained that he had attended grade school in Brownsville, Texas, but that his mother had taken the children over the bridge into Mexico after their father, a Texan, died. Along the bridge was a separate, cordoned-off lane for foot traffic, which whenever they had wanted to, the family had walked back and forth on all of their lives, so it wasn't as if they had needed to grow accustomed to being Mexican again. His mother still worked in Brownsville at a dry-cleaning establishment, and his sister and brother-in-law had opened an ice cream parlor just next door, so whenever Señor Fentin felt scruffy and malnourished, he went back for a cone and a pressing. He was the ugly duckling of the family, he told the Saulks with a self-mocking grin. But his teeth weren't half as bad as he made them out to be, and though the charter fishing trips were how he made his living, he smelled of sun-baked straw. He was twenty-nine, unmarried. When they left him on the road outside the hotel and went up to their room to change into appropriate boating clothes, they heard him chatting on the sidewalk with whoever passed by, in English and in Spanish, lighting people's cigarettes. The scent of lighter fluid and tobacco drifted in through the window. Finally it was this, the luxuriant idea of his cupping a lighter to their cigarettes out on the glittery open gulf, that kept them from changing their minds and having a siesta instead.

"I really wanted the nap," Jenessa's dad might say when, at a dinner with friends or on the phone with an uncle, he reached this part of the story. "I was happy to let him stay where he was. When you took off the bracelet, that's what I hoped you were saying to me."

"And I was such an ignoramus!" Jenessa's mom would answer.

Feeling it imprudent to take such a valuable object onto the water, Mrs. Saulk had laid the heavy silver bracelet link by link across the dresser top. Each flat, solid link was fashioned into a poppy, and in the absence of the silver her arm turned thin and girlish, a sapling of an arm. On second thought, she removed her watch as well and zipped the gold watch and the bracelet along with the matching brooch into a pocket of her cosmetics bag and tucked the bag beneath the invisible flap in the suitcase, next to the passports. Then she put on a zippered, canvas jacket, her formidable tortoiseshell sunglasses, and the same hat she'd been wearing before.

"Why wouldn't you put on your bathing suit under your clothes? I really wanted to watch," Jenessa's dad liked to ask.

"Why didn't *you* put on *your* bathing suit? Piggy."

Outside, Señor Fentin had managed to come up with a car, and he stood at the open passenger door to usher them grandly in. The backseat was crowded with disarranged road maps, and the car's owner, a second cousin of Fentin's wearing wire-rimmed spectacles, waved good-bye from a shop. On the dashboard sat a lumpy, misshapen fruit the Saulks didn't recognize, wearing identical spectacles, and slung over the seat was a striped necktie, which Fentin knotted one-handed on top of his polo collar while driving, completing the knot as soon as he'd parked the car at the docks. Now that the trip was under way he was less garrulous than before, preferring, it appeared, to crack subtle jokes at his own expense. He even seemed a little angry. With exaggerated gallantry he led them to the boat, which had an outboard motor and a makeshift canopy in case the sun was too strong. Some fishing gear lay in the bottom of the boat, where the paint had been rubbed away by other people's shoes. On each splintery bench sat a life jacket. Not until the boat had been chugging along for a good fifteen minutes did Jenessa's parents, who had little experience boating, recognize that it wasn't a sailboat, after all. There wasn't a mast or a boom. There was only the motor and rudder, and strapped to the gunwale were two oars of entirely different sizes, one as tall as Señor Fentin, one no longer than his arm.

After a few more minutes, they came to some buoys where brown pelicans perched. Brown pelicans were sillier looking than white ones, Mrs. Saulk observed. Every so often one of them flapped off into the sky, hovered around for a couple of seconds, saw no sign of lunch, then glided dispiritedly back to a buoy again. Señor Fentin stopped the motor anyway, and pulled out the dented tackle box. It was easier to run a charter service out of Mexico than out of the States, he explained, for there were more tourists in Mexico and far fewer regulations.

Like not being permitted to put a picture of a sailboat on your business card when your skiff had been folded that morning out of somebody's breakfast newspaper, Jenessa's dad thought. Already he worried that he was being taken advantage of. He couldn't tell yet. It wasn't so awful to be out on the gulf, sails or not, and they were having an outing, which was probably better than whiling away the final honeymoon hours on the hotel terrace, even though they had left the camera behind in the room by mistake.

But he wasn't a sturdy person, Jenessa's dad, and each time this fact was brought to his attention—by someone eating off his plate, by missing a softball that one of the neighborhood children tossed in his direction, or by pressing the wrong elevator button and walking off by mistake into a parking garage—he suffered anew with the affront. It wasn't the parking garage itself that hurt him, nor even, much later, the terrible truth about Señor Fentin. Instead it was the fact of Mr. Saulk not being even ordinarily brave. He couldn't *buck up*.

You have no inner resources, certain events announced to him, and each time the announcement was made, he yielded openly, raggedly to it. Jenessa's mom could undo him simply by creeping up behind him and blowing into his ear with the whistle in the shape of a bird, even if she did this once or twice a week. Jenessa too could undo him, and though she scrupulously avoided the whistle, the idea that she might bring tears to her dad's eyes simply by getting her own finger slammed in a door remained forever a burden to her.

"I don't understand this," Fentin remarked. "The fish are always ravenous here in this spot. But in a while we'll try that rectangular rock, out that way. That's where I go when they don't bite here."

When they examined this statement later on, it didn't exactly add up, but as they chugged in the direction of the rectangular-shaped rock, which from this distance resembled a floating house, Mrs. Saulk slid her arms from the sleeves of her jacket, tugged the jacket out from under the straps of her life jacket, pulled the cigarettes out of the jacket pocket, and distributed them around. The waves barely spanked the painted cradle of the boat, and the rock came so steadily nearer that they might as well have been speeding toward it in a convertible along a clean, paved road back home on Long Island. It might even resemble their own house, they thought, which they hadn't bought yet but they would, someday. When they reached the rock, it turned out to be a small house rather than a big, imposing one, but enormous as well because of the part that was hidden from them underwater.

Fentin shut off the motor, and used the longer of the two oars to keep the boat from smashing into the rock and the shorter of the oars to keep from straying too far away from it. His anchor had been stolen back in April, he apologized. At the top of the rock stood a sociable gathering of pelicans, which took turns plummeting past the boat and popping up seconds later with fish in their bills.

But the Saulks weren't as lucky. Nothing bit. They sat a full half hour, enjoying their cigarettes and sharing a couple of surprisingly cold beers that Fentin pulled from the tackle box and swiped clean with his shirt. There was no way of knowing, simply by looking at the rock, how far down it went.

"All the way to the bottom," Fentin asserted.

Finally they stowed the fishing gear back where it belonged, sliding the poles under the benches as Fentin pulled at the starter cord. The motor didn't come on. Through Fentin's binoculars, the streets of the town—a lazy commotion of traffic, the open square, the enviable roofline of the fancy hotel that didn't let in Jews—could be seen quite clearly, as could a few boats, none moving in their direction. Fentin pulled the cord again, and again there was nothing. Mrs. Saulk needed to go to the bathroom.

"So why don't you have a *Texas* accent, either? A *Southern* one," she asked Fentin, to distract herself.

"I have Mexican accent if somebody want me to," he answered after a moment, still fiddling with the motor. "Sometimes boat she is temperamental. No worry. Is no El Shark-O here this Time-O. But sometimes is little bit pain in the neck."

A pelican sent up a mighty splash. Fentin pulled the cord a third time, a muscle flexing in his arm. The motor whirred to life and got them to shore, where that evening at dinner Mrs. Saulk, who felt a little sick from the beer and the sun and the rocking to and fro, ate hardly a thing. But later on in the hotel room was when Jenessa was conceived.

"*Made*, like a sopaipilla with honey," went that part of the story. "Next day we flew home."

And then they rented the upstairs apartment in the skinny yellow house off Nathan Hale Road.

MRS. SAULK DIDN'T HAVE a difficult labor and delivery, exactly, except that it lasted for twenty-nine hours. During the contractions she shouted a mixture of complaint and exultation at the cold white ceiling, sort of a plea, or a curse, about labor. One of the labor-room staffers jotted down the words and later submitted this curious document to the in-house hospital newsletter, which printed it up in the form of a poem for inclusion on the patient bulletin page. Mrs. Saulk was pleased, though she could see that the poem was incorrect. It didn't breathe right, she realized instinctually. She didn't know poems. She'd never written one before and had read just a few while browsing in bookstores. But the breaks in her poem were in the wrong places. Either they didn't make sense, or they made too much sense. With the questionable help of the stout Mrs. Greene, the nurse the Saulks had hired to help out in the apartment after Jenessa was born, she set out to rearrange the poem by trial and error, writing it in longhand on one, two, and finally three sheets of paper, for it got longer the more liberally she broke the lines, and then she would stand in the center of the room to read each version aloud, marking the line breaks with discrete fluctuations in voice and tempo. Mrs. Greene liked the one that took up three sheets of paper the best, because of the way the pages were turned, each with a formal, whispery flourish. A private audience of two, she and the baby held very still in the crooked-runged rocker, being careful not to disrupt Mrs. Saulk's rhythm by setting up a contradictory beat of their own.

Over the days, other poems followed the one about labor; in fact, she wrote new ones all the time. There was the one she wrote about wearing her nightgown all day long and being clumsy because of it, *like a dreamer half-roused, half-flannel,* and another about her thumb being pricked by a diaper pin and becoming *the red hand of nap time.*

"That one really gets you on your toes," Mrs. Greene might offer obtusely, her neck reddening. Or, more helpfully, "Why is it always a *silvery* light? It shouldn't be, always."

Unfortunately, Mrs. Greene's role as critic only complicated matters insofar as her being the nurse. For one thing, she wasn't an actual nurse, only a sort of caretaker. If there was something nurselike that needed doing, like taking Jenessa's temperature or suctioning mucus out of her nostrils, Mrs. Greene declined involvement, arguing that she wasn't properly trained; and if there was something housekeeperly that needed doing, like mopping the floor, she resented being asked because she was really the babysitter.

The most she would do was swab Jenessa's cradle cap with baby oil and launder the baby clothes, filling whole mornings with the ironing of diapers while scolding Mrs. Saulk for having elected to breast-feed.

"What if you run out of milk?" she would admonish, her housedress straining at the armpits. "What will the baby think of its mother then?"

The only way to make her quit scolding was to wonder aloud who would sterilize the baby bottles and boil the nipples, causing Mrs. Greene to remember something that needed doing down on the porch. Sometimes she swept the porch gladly enough, but other times she balked at merely bringing in the newspaper. No matter what, Mrs. Greene would somehow manage to get locked out. Even fetching the mail, she would be locked out. And when the milk was delivered or it was time to bring the empty bottles down to the box, she would get locked out again. Usually she stayed there for a couple of minutes before pulling the bell on the end of the rope, from Mexico, to be let in, and after a while it seemed that that was why she locked herself out in the first place, in order to be justified in ringing the bell. She grew up on a farm, Mr. Saulk concluded with utmost certainty when he was telling the story, though Mrs. Saulk pointed out that really they knew almost nothing about her.

Aside from providing an attentive audience for poems, the ability to give Jenessa her daily bath turned out to be Mrs. Greene's primary qualification. Every day she gave a fun kitchen-sink bath, sliding the dirty dishes out of reach along the counter in order to clear enough space to play. Afterward she laid the naked baby on her lap and blew a steady stream of air back and forth along her body, tickling Jenessa like crazy while at the same time preventing diaper rash.

After Jenessa was diapered and dressed, Mrs. Saulk liked to lie on the couch with her daughter at rest on top of her, belly to belly. In this way mother and child often fell asleep reading the newspaper, which made a pup tent above them. The two of them were just dozing off like this one afternoon when someone came to the door, so Mrs. Greene, who was fluffing the towels on the rods in the bathroom (she seemed to do this twice a day), went down to the porch to answer it. The door clicked shut behind her, and after that, there was the usual period of almost preternatural quiet, during which Mrs. Saulk had a nightmare that turned out to be a genuine thing that was really happening. That is, she kept seeing Señor Fentin's handsome face floating in front of her. Before dozing off, she had been thinking about there being too many *like*s in poetry. Why was everything always *like* something else, in a poem? Nothing ever just *was*, she said to herself, half closing her eyes on the woozy canopy of newsprint and seeing Señor Fentin materialize before her. Paul Newman, when he starred some years later in *Butch Cassidy and the Sundance Kid*, would remind her of him. Her head propped on a cushion, she forced her eyes open, then let them drift heavily shut, then opened and shut them again, spinning loose for a while around the bothersome noise of the clanging, clanging bell, which was Mrs. Greene demanding to be let in.

"Oh, just stay the heck out there," Jenessa's mom murmured, tired of climbing up and down stairs and still being the one who rinsed out the diapers. Now that she thought about it, she discovered that she didn't object to diapers, feeling that the ordinary chores of motherhood kept her poems, diaphanous as they often were, rooted in the sticky, muddy business of everyday living.

"We should just find a regular babysitter who shows up when we want her and goes away when we don't," she decided, stroking Jenessa's waffle-weave onesie. The sleeping baby's bottom rose and fell in exact counterpoint to her mom's breathing. Señor Fentin had no mustache now. That was the only thing different about him from when he had taken them fishing. The bell kept ringing, *like cotton*, Mrs. Saulk said sleepily to herself, annoyed—*ringing like cotton?*—and let the newspaper settle on top of Jenessa, a blurred shadow sliding between paper and child.

Some time later, Jenessa startled, waking her. All was quiet outside on the porch, where the clanging had ceased. Mrs. Saulk sat up with Jenessa in her arms, picked up the newspaper, and found herself blinking at Señor Fentin's face. Yes, it was him. There was even his name, Eduard Fentin, charter fisherman . . . who had murdered a pair of newlyweds from Newport, Rhode Island, a week earlier. He had taken them out on his boat to fish, hit them with an oar, strangled them with a necktie, stolen their jewelry along with their camera, and dumped the bodies overboard. There was a portrait of the victims cutting the cake at their fancy Newport wedding, their knuckles flecked with frosting. There was also a picture of the house-shaped rock on the glistening water, the pelicans conferring up on the roofline.

For three reasons, Jenessa's dad sent flowers to his wife on the day Señor Fentin appeared in the paper. The main reason was that her nipples were sore from nursing, and he wanted her to know that he supported her decision to breast-feed even though Mrs. Greene looked askance at her for doing so. The second reason was to celebrate Jenessa's three-month birthday, and the third reason was that he wanted to do his part in keeping the local flower shop in business. There wasn't an obvious reason for fearing it might close, for it occupied a well-traveled corner in a prosperous part of town, but there were so many fresh flowers in the window every day, it seemed impossible that enough people would buy them.

He selected snapdragons, thinking it might be fun to show Jenessa their funny-looking mouths opening and closing. Watchfully, he supervised the wrapping of the flowers in a stiff cone of paper, paying a little extra for delivery. He expected that the nurse would stand them in a vase in the kitchen, so he was surprised when he got home that evening to find the table bare, empty even of place settings, and Mrs. Greene, who ordinarily left at six, nowhere in sight. Instead he was greeted by a wide-eyed Jenessa supine in her playpen, pedaling the air, and Mrs. Saulk at the stove, preparing a supper of chipped beef on toast.

Turning to greet him, she was flushed and excited. "Señor Fentin bludgeoned to death a pair of Newport honeymooners and dumped their bodies overboard at the rock we fished at!" she exclaimed, holding out the newspaper for him to see, then imitating his shocked expressions one after the other as he read the article. The body of the bride had washed onto a beach, but the groom was still somewhere out there. Fentin had been found with one of the wristwatches still in his possession and had shortly confessed.

Mrs. Saulk dished out two plates of food, handing the rinsed-off spoon to the baby to be banged on the floor. Dinner was over before Mr. Saulk remembered the wrapped snapdragons. At first, he couldn't bring himself to mention them. It didn't seem right. You could pick snapdragons off the side of the road in some places if you wanted. You could pick roses too, if you were alive.

But finally he asked. Had there been anything delivered to the house that day?

"Oh!" Jenessa's mom answered. "Mrs. Greene didn't come back in! I mean I'm not going to keep on letting her back in every other minute. As far as I'm concerned she can stay out there forever, find another dozen eggs to make her famous egg salad one day a week."

It was funny how little they knew of Mrs. Greene, the Saulks speculated in bed that evening, after lovemaking probably, although Jenessa, when she was grown, just imagined this part: her dad's hand quiet on her mom's bare shoulder as the two of them lay there talking. And when her mom gave a shrug, the hand slid off. And when he put the hand back on again, again she shimmied it off, like not letting Mrs. Greene back into the house. Mrs. Greene must have taken the snapdragons with her, and she had stolen the bell but had left behind the rope. How old was the housekeeper? They'd never asked. Where on earth had she been raised? Was she married? Was she a mother? Had she graduated high school? Did she even have a name? Yes, it was Erma.

Henry Kissinger's brother lived on Lower Drive, on the way to Jenessa's kindergarten bus stop, which occupied a grass island at the juncture of Upper Drive and Cove Road, not far from where the Saulks had finally purchased their house. The Saulks, who weren't as well-heeled as a lot of their neighbors, had bought a modest Cape Cod constructed back when the estates had been parceled off. Still, they liked the stony glamour of their surroundings, Jenessa's mom because it made their own house appear nobler than it was, and Jenessa's dad because the sight of the Kissinger manor with its cracked tile roof, and of the yellowing Tudor where Betty Grable supposedly sometimes stayed, made him feel that his family was safe and protected. Neither Upper nor Lower Drive was paved, but what with the derelict mansions and cloisterly trees, the neighborhood gave off a knighted air that felt separate from ordinary time. Cove Road, flecked with mica, fell in a gradual slant to the beach, coming to a stop near the cluster of sandy Bay Club cabanas within sight of what would soon become the singer Harry Chapin's house. For a long time, the Bay Club didn't let in Jews, and when it finally did, Mrs. Saulk felt gaily vindicated in refusing their invitation to join.

In 1967, when Jenessa had just turned seven and was walking to her bus stop one day, a stranger pulled alongside her in his car, kneed open the door, and reached so near that his fingertips grazed the fringes of her knitted, toggled cape.

"Here, *girlie!* Wanna ride?" he called.

Jenessa shook her head no at the man's thick fingers and stepped with finality out of his reach. Her babysitter, Mrs. Kribs, had trained her to do this.

"What if somebody you don't know, somebody you've never even seen before, asks you to get in their car? What will you do?" the bright sixty-year-old lady sometimes quizzed

Jenessa. "And if they offer you candy or toys? Or candy *and* toys? What will you do then?"

When the car slowed beside her, Jenessa had only been ambling along, kicking at some fallen tulip-tree pods, but at once she started walking as Mrs. Kribs had taught her, *like a sewing machine needle stitching a hem,* glancing neither right nor left. Past the sledding hill she went, to where the pavement turned to dirt on Lower Drive before it reached the Cove Road bus stop.

Later, home from school, she told Mrs. Kribs about it. Jenessa's dad was at work. Mrs. Saulk was upstairs in her dormer-room office, tapping out syllables. Her book of poems was going to be published, so her muffled recitations of them drifted through the house at all hours, day and night.

"Are there any other little girls who walk with you to that bus stop?" Mrs. Kribs asked, squatting for a better look at Jenessa, and to undo the toggles of the knitted cape.

"Betsy Rassmusen, but she never catches up."

Quickly Mrs. Kribs telephoned Mrs. Rassmusen, craning her neck in the direction of the window to wave merrily at a car pulling into the drive. She was expert at doing two or three things at once. She was always well-groomed, always wearing pumps no matter what time of day. Widowed in her forties, she was at last to remarry *a septuagenarian,* as she liked to say, and was to leave the apartment she shared with her daughter and move into a new one in a smart brick building right next to the public library. She spoke very little of her husband-to-be, whose name was Mr. Anderssen, but when she did, she always lost her composure for a couple of seconds, her excitement riffling the pretty margins of her person, as if a song had started coming to her out of the air and then settled around her cardigan sweater.

That afternoon, the three of them—Mrs. Kribs, Jenessa, and Mr. Anderssen—were to go for a drive, transporting a large, potted avocado tree from Mrs. Kribs's daughter's front hallway to the breakfast nook of the new apartment, and it was he, Mr. Anderssen, who was just pulling up in the Saulks' gravel drive, honking his horn in greeting before stepping along the path to the door.

"Now what color car did you say tried to scare you and Betsy this morning? And would you bring me that blanket from the rocker, dear, to spread over the car seat? To protect it from the potting soil," Mrs. Kribs said to Jenessa from over the tilt of the telephone receiver. And then, into the phone, "I'm glad Betsy's just fine."

"The car was brown," Jenessa answered. "It was covered in rust."

This was strictly untrue, but she was too stunned to say that the car had been white, the same clean, polished white as was the car parked in the driveway, and that the man at the threshold was the very same man, with the meaty, scrubbed fingers and buttoned-up shirt cuffs, and even the same high, embarrassing voice. He didn't call her *girlie* this time, of course. He said, "Well, well, Jenessa, I've heard so much about you," not showing that he recognized her from earlier that day. And maybe he didn't, for she had taken off her cape, and she was holding the Mexican blanket now, black with red lines in the pattern of a maze. Her sneakers were dented, her hair maybe a little mussed. Jenessa had a feeling, whenever she came back to this moment—a feeling that scrolled out over the years, under her skin. It had to do with Mexico. There wasn't the word, *Mexico;* there was only a thing that was going on in secret in another, hidden chapter of her parents' favorite story, a part that only she could tell, about another little girl with the same long hair as Jenessa, worn like a set of draperies, so that she looked like a girl stepping out from between the two halves of herself, the twinned possibilities.

Mrs. Kribs took the blanket, swept at a crease with the palm of her hand, and led the way to the driveway, stepping carefully along on the bricks in her pumps. Jenessa refused to get into Mr. Anderssen's shiny white car. She didn't feel good, she explained. The blanket's maze made her dizzy as she watched it unfold across the backseat. Just beyond lay the woods, a phalanx of ash tree and oak. Squirrels took aim at your head if you walked underneath, the acorns thonking to the ground. There was a Midge doll in a barbecue outfit lost in those woods, about which Jenessa's mom was writing a poem and happened to need, at that very moment, a piece of advice. With her fingernails she rapped on the dormer-room window, beckoning Jenessa back into the house.

"The Midge doll," she inquired, not swiveling in her swivel chair to face her daughter. "Is she wearing a sundress?"

Jenessa was accustomed to her mom's silhouette, her mom's eyes trained on the typewriter paper, her mom's hands readying themselves in the space above the keys. And she had learned to appreciate this view of her mom, her unspoken acknowledgment of Jenessa, Jenessa panting in the doorway after running quickly upstairs, like a pact they shared.

THE BELL AT THE END OF A ROPE

There rose a fan of spun gravel outside on the driveway—Mrs. Kribs and Mr. Anderssen speeding off to their apartment.

"Pedal pushers," Jenessa replied.

IN A ROOM NEAR THE DORMER-ROOM OFFICE sat a small TV with a tilted antenna, and it was through this TV, so Jenessa's parents' story went, that the news of the world first reached the Saulk household, like when Martin Luther King Jr. was shot, and after that Bobby Kennedy, and just a short time later, Erma Greene the nurse, who wasn't shot but arrested for drowning two newborns in two separate kitchen sinks on two separate occasions, forgetting that they were in there while she went to fetch the mail. Jenessa's dad was bouncing Jenessa's new tiny rubber Super Ball when Erma Greene's clompy shoes first appeared on TV, the backs of her knees two wide pale strips between the hem of her skirt and the tops of her socks. The rubber ball struck the ceiling, ricocheted against the eaves, and was gone eleven months, to be finally discovered wedged beneath the keys of Jenessa's mom's typewriter, blocking only the capital letter *I*.

"Who wants casserole?" Jenessa's mom announced at dinner. "Does Jenessa want casserole? Does Steve want casserole? Does the lady who is standing here waving the serving spoon want casserole? Jenessa, can you see your dad hates it when your mom refers to herself like this in the third person? He does, you know. It makes him feel abandoned."

After that, if her dad was at work and her mom had flown off on one of her poetry tours, Jenessa had the curious feeling of not knowing which of her parents might arrive first to claim her—her real mother and father, or her other sort-of parents, Señor Fentin, Mrs. Greene, and Mr. Anderssen, who seemed to hover out of sight as if to follow her around. They carried the blanket, and the bell that had been stolen from the end of the rope, but they had left her the skeleton perched on the painted chair, its rib cage peeling, the plaster flaking into bits as the years went by. Its name was Ed, short for El Día de los Muertos, but when Jenessa started college in upstate New York to study math, which she loved for its subtle equations, its way of grouping together and singling apart, she took only the chair, which sat quietly in her room as if waiting for new things to come to pass.

For some time, not much did, though Harry Chapin, of course, died in that crash on the Long Island Expressway. And all along the name *Erma* had been crouching inside of the word *fisherman,* Jenessa realized with a prickle of apprehension one morning while driving to work, when she was practically already married to a man she had been courting in a most brazen manner even though she hardly knew him. In fact, he was scary. But then, wasn't everybody? So when she was flicking her fog lights that morning and felt the prickly sensation, she didn't swivel to look behind her at the road, she didn't step on the brakes, and she didn't speed up. Instead she thought about how things change in a minute but also how even before she was born she had managed to step past those minutes with only the smallest amount of effort. So she kept on driving and thought about home on Long Island, where the Bay Club was crumbling and the Cape Cod house hunkered ever more deeply under the leathery pods of the trees. She hadn't been there in a while, but she could see it in her mind: her mom's restless fingers typing at air, her dad scrunching his eyebrows under the sheets, hating for his dreams to be interrupted.

ERASURES

ONLY WHEN SANDRA is passing through security this morning does she discover he has finally stolen her wallet. They've been waiting, complicit, for him to do this. First he stole quarters, then dollars, then twenties, and each time, from their distance in the apartment, she sensed him sensing her finding him out: her riffling her bills, double-checking the inner breast pocket of her interview blazer, then hiding a ten in her underwear drawer but saying nothing about it when they met later over lamb chops and cauliflower, the twin chops on the platter inclined like their brows at the dinner table. So closely had he followed the recipe in his cookbook that the salads exactly matched the book's cottage-cheese-and-pear-rabbit photo. He nibbled first at the ears, she at the feet, him sensing her sensing him sensing her not accusing him of theft. It makes her smug to feel this close to her son. She likes to fight against the smugness and feel herself lose the argument. He must know she tends to carry her passport with her even on these briefest of interview jogs, for if he didn't, he would never have stolen the wallet.

    She takes her place at the gate and arranges herself in her interview trousers and arrestingly slender interview sweater, aware of what generous hips she's got and how slender the rest of her perching above, as if she might slip through them, birthing herself, her eyes gluey with wonderment at having her own self for a mother as well as a daughter, her son a brother as well as a thief. Remarking on the lightness of her carry-on while pulling it down the ramp for boarding, Sandra lurches to a halt, realizing he's stolen her laptop as well, the little Gateway she'd bought with her postdivorce assets. The Gateway contains all of her interview seminar notes as well as, separately, inside its foamy, zippered sleeve, the book of poems that, to the boy's credit, he would have had no idea was packed in there. If he knew it, he wouldn't have stolen it. Purportedly, it's her second book. She had written those poems before she was married, months before she was even pregnant with him. The manuscript had won a competition and been published by a fine university press, receiving acclaim just modest enough that when she published the identical manuscript under a new title (the first was *Eventide*, the second *High Tide Fanciful*) at a different press two years after the first press closed, nobody noticed that it was the same. And then, when a third press awarded the manuscript *its* prize twenty-eight months later, offering a self-congratulatory apology for having taken so long to consider it, she decided that the third press had earned this accidental right to fulfill her need for a third publication on which her salary depended. But then the job dried up anyway.

ERASURES

As for her fourth book, she hasn't yet decided what kind of approach to take to it. The problem, she worries, rolling her boarding pass into a secretive sort of breathing straw between her thumb and index finger as she pauses on the ramp, aware of other airline passengers maneuvering their luggage around her bountiful hips, is that she is required to read from that fourth, unwritten poetry book at tonight's event.

For a moment she considers not boarding the plane and forgoing the interview altogether. The old manuscript—the one that became book one, book two, and book three—is nowhere online, and there will be no time to search at a library. Does she even remember a line or two? Maybe a stanza. In a burst of maternal, preemptive forgiveness, she tilts the carry-on onto its back, like a baby needing changing right there on the ramp, and checks all the zippered pouches in case her son had thought to zip the book somewhere else, but the only thing she finds is that he's stolen her eyeglasses too. She imagines the glasses sightless in a drawer of the dresser in his dad's big house on Bowen Street, filled with clothes the boy won't wear. He's not a bad man, her ex, and she had never meant to hurt him. He simply doesn't have a clue what clothes to buy.

On the plane, she hefts the carry-on into the overhead, but when she calls her son's cell phone, nobody answers. Nor does his dad, either at his fancy office or at the house on Bowen Street, three miles from her apartment and ten times bigger, which is where the boy stays whenever she's gone. After breakfast that morning, before she drove him to his dad's to drop off his bag and then took him to school on her way to the airport, she reminded the boy, as she does for every trip to every interview, that she has left him some kisses, "one for morning, one for night, and one for morning again." Then she showed him the vase with the kisses inside, a fist-size vase with the wine-cork stopper. Sensing his worry, and him sensing her sensing him sensing *her* worry, she planted some extra kisses in it for after school.

"They do like to try to escape," she warned, pressing the stopper back in as quick as could be, "but they're not very fast." Together, they loaded their suitcases into the car. It must have been when they were driving to his dad's that he smuggled her wallet and laptop out of her luggage into his own, and then the eyeglasses, trapped in their too-snug case. From the window after takeoff, the lake looks like an iced-over cup of milk. The pelicans have flown south, but the geese, which are late this year in departing, veer in panicky Vs past the flats. Her boy likes his milk frozen. It's the only way he'll drink it. His dad often forgets and serves it too warm, although he isn't rash, careless, or in the least untrustworthy. Although she'd never meant to hurt him, the dad cries too much, blotting his tears on tablecloth hems.

She slides her feet from her clogs, and wonders: What will she "present" at her reading tonight, without her book of poems? And what will she teach, without the laptop notes for her sample seminar? Absently she squints at this seemingly far-off question, wondering how worrisome other mothers might find it to have a son who steals from her even her chances of finding a job, a wage, a pension, even her wallet with her Free Dozen Bagels card ready for swapping, as if to prepare her for the usual hunger she feels on planes, the feeling, from being in transit, of being groundless, without gravity or mass, without even her footwear, which have skidded too far underneath the seat ahead of her. Once, when she was married but before her son was born, she left her husband in a bar where there was in progress a noisy, cold party, and crossed the street in new rain to a coffee shop. She sat for an hour as the storm lashed the window in which the CLOSED sign faced her, as if it were the sidewalk beyond the window that was closed to her. The neighborhood, closed. The bar with the crowded party, closed. The highway overpass, closed. She remembers she shut her eyes in relief, sipping her coffee, the whole rest of the world forbidden her. Flying feels like that. Even the limo driver who comes to meet her outside baggage claim appears to be in on it, crossing her name off a list on his clipboard, and so does the girl with the keys at the counter in the foyer of the dormitory in which Sandra's been put for her overnight stay. She phones her son and her ex from the limo, then from the stairway, then from the hallway, the kind of journey into which a rat might be dropped for intelligence testing.

 With the ungainly dormitory key, which is attached by a small length of chain to a block of wood, she unlocks her door. There's a desk built out of the same wood. A glacier wouldn't budge it. But in the drawer lies a book by an up-and-coming poet, so she practices reading aloud from it, haltingly, since she has no glasses, and with an air of startled vagueness, since she doesn't really understand the work. In this way, reading a stranger's inscrutable poetry, she gets through the night's public event, squinting at the book laid flat on the podium as if with the ur-memory of having written such lines, thankfully unable to meet the eyes of her audience, since she can barely see their faces without her glasses. Having promised to look for boys her son's age, she finds one who sinks all the deeper into his seat when it's time for applause. The ovation astounds her, as do the tears amid the audience members, since she really doesn't like to make people cry. She would rather inspire them to take off their clothes, or forget to eat, or neglect their responsibilities.

At every reasonable juncture for the rest of her visit, even during her seminar, at which she urges the class to compose *erasures*, using random writings they happen to have in their backpacks, erasing fragments of text so as to leave chosen phrases and words exposed, Sandra calls her son, but the boy doesn't answer. Nor does the dad; he of Bob Dylan's *Christmas in the Heart* CD and bagels and lox on Christmas mornings, he who still pays the health insurance.

As if feeling ungrateful not to have gotten sick at least some of the time and made use of her ex-husband's insufferable generosity in providing health insurance, Sandra sniffles and coughs all the way to the airport, then snoozes away, her face at the window, her clogs out of reach, missing the dusky white view of the ice. Erasures are really just literary parlor games, she secretly believes, although they do have a way of posing sly alternatives to the pages in question, like the time she was stuck in that coffee shop and the rest of the world was denied her, and like when she arrives at the dad's dark house on Bowen Street and unlocks the door with the key he has given her, and finds the whole house empty. There's not a stick of furniture, no couch, nor desk, nor chair, not even the boy's dresser with the clothes he won't wear. The only thing left is her laptop, in the kitchen, aglow with a message typed by the dad.

ERASURES

I DO MEAN TO HURT YOU, the message reads.

She stands still a long while as if critiquing a poem, one she can hardly be expected to be able to make adequate sense of without her glasses. Even blind she can tell it's not such a great poem. Most poems are much better. So she deletes it.

QUINT

LIKE I DO ON OTHER MORNINGS, I knot the laces of my sneakers, choose the hand-knitted sweater with those cheerful clock-face buttons, button you up, and sit you square in the stroller with your fresh chili pepper for gumming and chewing. The stem curls amid your fingers like a slender pepper-finger, all digits entwined. Though I would never've guessed you'd bliss out on chilies, it seems like I might have. You, fretful all week with the pain of the teething, flipping chew toys right and left, bending over—"like a paperclip," I mention to your father—to gnaw on the padded stroller bar. Us—you and me—strolling home from IGA with the paper sack of groceries perched on your lap. Me, pausing to explain, even though you aren't yet walking, the rudiments of street crossing. You'd pulled a chili from the sack and sat speculatively, vexedly nursing at it, your eyes pinkly amused by the sting and its comforts, stumping me. Every morning since then, I rinse a fresh chili pepper, double-check it for bruises, blot it on a tea towel, and weave the stem among your fingers, awash in your spit, anointed by drool.

"Can you tell me four reasons for which we stop at each corner?" I inquire of you this morning, even though you are way too young to talk:

1. because in moving through life we carry our safety in our own hands; and
2. because although there is harm that we can't see coming, or couldn't stop it even if we did see it coming, or maybe should not try to stop it, so too are there dangers we strive to avoid; and
3. because although you are mine, we are each of us secured, for better or worse, inside our own bodies, our selves swimming like fish in precarious bowls, bowls that
4. we must handle with care while hazarding streets immaterial and material.

Although you are way too young to count, I count these reasons on my fingers so as to teach you the numbers *one, two, three,* and *four,* for earth, air, fire, and water, the fundamental unheavenly elements, the street empty of traffic for visible miles in both flat directions, but still we stop at the curbside, you and me, looking both ways while you pause in your suckling to point with the chili toward the place where you know we are headed, which, because we come here every day, you recognize at once, although you're too small even to hope for or anticipate it—the little park beside the reservoir, the footpath stained with mulberries near the vast, oval lawn where people gather on Fourths of July to watch fireworks, but where today there is nobody yet but us, because it is not yet ten o'clock.

"You're not too young to *count*. You're too young to *count*," I apologize, recalling some news clip from NPR about how babies know more than their mothers think they do. Babies know exactly what's really going on and they can do statistics with Ping-Pong balls. As I mentioned to your father while smoothing the frizz from his ponytail while he and I lay spooning across the hallway from your crib, these daily walks around the reservoir are our "most educational enterprise." People fish here some days, and once, when we admired a bait pail of crawfish in view of which I recited for you that quadrille:

> *Would not, could not, would not, could not, would not join the dance.*
> *Would not, could not, would not, could not, could not join the dance,*

the fisherman plucked out the plumpest crawfish and snapped it in half like a roll of quarters. Another time, when we had paused in our strolling to watch a ground squirrel cross the footpath, a cat darted out from the mulberry trees, pounced on the squirrel, punctured its neck, bit off its ear, and trotted back into the woods with it dangling from its mouth. You remained as unperturbed by these grisly events as if they were skits on Saturday a.m. television, whether because since everything was new to you everything was ordinary, or because since everything was new to you everything was extraordinary, you were way too young to say.

Now you join me a moment in frowning back in the direction from which we came, where, past the lopsided stones of the tipped-over tower, footsteps stir amid the gravel, most unwelcome footsteps, being not the right ones, because it is not quite ten o'clock. I feign not looking not dreading not waiting not minding not despairing not paying attention. Even so, Lanette Silber, neighborhood gossip, colleague of your father, veers in our direction, picking grass stems as she comes, for braiding lanyards with. I've watched her do this at potlucks, the lanyards tidy and green, Lanette dipping one into her glass of iced tea before sipping it dry but today stooping gently to gift the handicraft to you, extending it past the embarrassing clump of our resourceful pacifier, that pulp that you have made of the heat from your chili pepper.

"Peppers have pharmaceutical properties," I explain.

"Here's a lanyard made of grass," Lanette Silber intervenes, the two speeches colliding above where you sit taste-testing, nibbling, and calibrating as if puzzling over a long first kiss. I hurt her once, Lanette, inexpressibly. I am often too blunt. I am tactless, thus cruel. I've been warned of this by friends and by your father, who reminds me that because I tend to harm people unintentionally, I must "practice thinking" before I open my mouth, allowing my thoughts to settle like tops after spinning so that we—he and I, your father and I—might measure the angles at which they have landed before I run the fateful risk of speaking aloud.

Lanette's baby died. It might have been your older playmate a year from now. Its cheeks were two apples, its small figure papoosed in a bright-blue blanket the last time I saw it when it was alive, when you weren't yet conceived. The three of them—Lanette and her husband and their new baby, the baby cradled like a football in its father's arms for a go around the park on a day some time before the mulberries formed, the path around the reservoir devoid of purple stains, the trees barely leafing, a breeze biting the tail of the snugly cinched blanket—paused on their stroll to chat with me. The baby died of meningitis one week later, and when I next saw Lanette—not including at the funeral, to which people carried baggies of goldfish for setting loose in a pond—here on this grassy but at the time muddy amphitheater, a handkerchief binding the knuckles of one of her hands, I asked her, "Will you have another baby?" as if offering a plate of mini quiches at a party, causing a reaction in the sky a sort of gulping of some clouds a shift in the migration of the four elements a reversion of sympathies the buds on the mulberries enacting their stasis, their dormancy. The handkerchief twisted tighter around Lanette's knuckles. She replied she didn't know. Soon we parted and went home. It's not unlikely she might harm me today in return, since it is just now ten o'clock.

"I read once," I tell her, "I read once in a cooking magazine that the spiciness of chili peppers comes from actual, physical, miniature daggers."

The two of us—Lanette and I—watch you flinch as you suck out the daggers then gum them then swallow them whole like swords. From past the toppled stone tower, footsteps come, sneakers on gravel. The sound is welcome and familiar and although you are way too young to know it, you really do seem to know it—the chili suspended, the lanyard drooping like a flower, your chapped grin inflamed even though you are innocent even of gladness. The figure pauses midstep, secures his balance, then advances on the balls of his feet like somebody miming his own approach. Of the fundamental elements only the fifth, the quintessence, remains pure, incorruptible. Hair silvering like a mirror, sweatshirt linty, the tall figure, gently creaking, bends for the daily handshake. "Good day, young fellow, and what are you and your sweet and ever-so-lovely mother up to on this neither ordinary nor extraordinary morning?"

But then, winking, he glides to where the footpath forks through the woods where the creek mucks through, past the bed of soft leaves where he likes us to sit "visiting."

I stand way too stoically watching him go, Lanette tattling, "I'm sorry," into my ear like mulberries falling onto the path. Then we—you and I—stroll on home, to where your father isn't waiting, since it is not yet time for lunch. I pull you out of the seat and you fuss then cry then wail then screech against me, the chili mashed to the floor in your first-ever tantrum, your strictest, your inconsolable rebuke of me.

TWO STRAIGHT WOMEN TALKING

1. Now that he's dead and she can smoke again she finds the thought untenable, the struck match the gray taste of him sliding in and out of her but no push or pull, no *yes*, no *ahh*, no body.

    No, she couldn't.

    "Not possible," she tells her friend, then takes the thing and keeps it unlit between her fingers, so slender, so eager to vanish, the flavor a memory, the effect turned to vapor every time she wants it most.

    "I can't stand it," is what he said, "the thought of you putting that thing, the idea of it, the smell of it, the children, I can't sleep with it I won't fuck you if you smoke it you bitch you idiot you stinking you killing yourself not smart not you not the mother of my children not the person I married."

TWO STRAIGHT WOMEN TALKING

So he slept in the room below hers, in the narrow bed reserved for visitors. That was her first night without him.

2. SHE USED TO DO IT in the woods near the bridge across the creek but not on the bridge, no, on a log that she straddled, then lit up then leaned back then watched the trees staying the same minute after minute not shrinking not burning up not turning to ash on the water. She knew he would hate it. The thought gave her pleasure as did the fact he didn't know it he hadn't figured it out he couldn't smell it when she got home she brushed her teeth slid the pack into a coat pocket in one of the closets, a secret, a dark hole so private she couldn't find herself in it. No, she found somebody else, some other woman, not his wife not the mother of his children not anyone he knew not someone her own mother would recognize draped in dark leathers sunglasses so big you could watch the woods in them the squirrels chirping the snapped twigs the white cat in dead leaves the surprise of each moment the sulfur the flame that was in her. No, this was not her, this woman with these yearnings this thing between her lips this half-formed smile.

3. ONCE, WHEN SHE WAS SITTING there smoking, she saw a man across the way, watching her. She recognized his clothing. He was the man who jogged past her car every morning never nodding never mouthing hello except now he gazed at her so perplexedly she wondered, How does he know me? How does he know I "don't smoke"? She stubbed the cigarette out on damp splinters of log then shoved the butt into the rot, buried it in sawdust she would smell on her fingertips days later.

THE BELL AT THE END OF A ROPE

When she glanced up he was gone. There was only the opposite edge of the creek you'd have to walk across air to get to and off in the trees a glimpse now and then of crimson Lycra and the high-flashing whites of his shoes. She wondered, Who am I if not the woman he sees every morning in her car on her way to work the children buckled in behind her the husband gesticulating lecturing pontificating into the sunlight?

4. How do I know, she inquired of her friend, whether I am the one who doesn't smoke or the one who does?

5. "How do I know," asked her husband, "that you're telling the truth?"

"The truth," she insisted, "the truth is two weeks. I've been smoking two weeks," although it felt like a whole new life her limbs pulsing with mischief and nicotine, her mouth stinking of toothpaste, Macintosh apples, tall, sharp glasses of grapefruit juice, whatever erased the evidence. That night it was a mint leaf snatched from among some weeds in the garden, hastily chewed, spat out, the cold mud of it gritty all over her teeth. He needed the car. Out to dinner they'd been, to some place in the city. When they got home she drove the babysitter back to the girl's parents' house on Hollywood Street then switched on the radio loud then cruised around searching for someplace to park. She'd been waiting all night for this moment the matches stolen from behind her husband's back when he ordered the beers. Over shrimp and lemongrass, coconut, and cilantro all she could taste was one long inhalation. Now the radio was singing, the night wet the roads slick, black, and empty.

TWO STRAIGHT WOMEN TALKING

So impatient was she that she blocked someone's driveway while parking then stayed where she was not caring not wanting to call attention to the way her hand shook as she opened the window, the lit end of the cigarette quaking with anticipation (This is stupid, she was thinking, to do it in the car he'll smell it he'll find the afterglow the scattered flecks on the upholstery the butt with her kiss on it wedged in the tire tread), but still the taste of it the endless drag of meditation. She smoked three, one after another, wondering slyly whose driveway she was blocking and if they thought they knew her. She wondered, Am I the kind who throws her stubs in the road or the kind who keeps them safe for incineration? She left the stubs in the ashtray kept the ashtray open so as not to forget to dump it in the trash when she got home. But he was standing on the lawn when she entered the driveway the children asleep the house dark behind him save for the hall leading into and out of his study the laptop tucked under his coat in the rain.

"I need the car I need to print out my memo," he said, the memo he'd recited to her over dinner the waiter eavesdropping even the olive oil weighing in on things but in a moment, "Who was smoking? Who was *smoking?*"

He yanked the ashtray from the dash, held it out at arm's length two-fingered the way men hold their condoms after removal, "So this is what you've been running around for this is what you've been sneaking around with this is what you've been keeping from me I knew it was something."

Later she supposed she might have blamed it on the babysitter though who would have believed it that young thing in pink kneesocks even her eyeglasses bright eyed from their studies of Uncertainty.

THE BELL AT THE END OF A ROPE

6. "I KNEW IT WAS SOMETHING," he said, "I knew it was something you were doing behind my back getting away with I can't believe it I can't stand it the tobacco companies those fat stinking money-sucking liars your business our money your lungs black already the thing already starting to happen the children the example the injustice of it the stupidity of it how could you who are you who do you think you are?"

7. NOW THE FACT OF IT the part that's indisputable the thing that can't be argued the slender reality of it the delicate compact heft of it the way it seemed to resist gravity so that even if she dropped it it fell slowly like a thing seen falling from a distance although of course she couldn't catch it there was no sound when it hit, just the sight of it the cylindrical void of it among the damp leaves the dark earth the scattered crushed berries. And then the shock of it once more between her fingers the satin of it the profound invitation.

8. ANOTHER FACT, an absolute, she could never get the match to flare with just one strike.
    "You can't?" asked her friend, also a mother the children playing in his study dumping files on the carpet pencils pens erasers and clips on the carpet discs on the carpet memo upon memo upon memo on the carpet she wouldn't find it till later the mountain of papers *we must we should we must never in the abstract one suspects statistically significant by my calculations indisputable we must not make the mistake of* an anthill the children had built on the carpet.
    "No," she said, she couldn't, three matches at least were required the aroma of sulfur the tip hot to the touch

before the flame was provoked and even then it might sputter prematurely leaving her unsatisfied her mouth empty her tongue frustrated her neck craned foolishly forward. And, she never knew quite what to do with each spent ineffectual match, slide it horizontally into the matchbook drop it in the cigarette pack slip it into her pocket toss it into the creek watch it travel away before permitting herself the luxury of the second, less-tenuous flame the way it burned her cupped fingers the way it singed her eyebrows if she had to bend close the way she never drew back even from the pain of it if she was getting what she wanted.

9. Black jeans leather jacket brown as the underside of a log black socks ankle boots with the glue gone bad in the soles green T-shirt dark wing-tipped glasses pushed to the crown of her head these were other facts in which she felt in equal doses camouflaged and entirely exposed like something the weather might enter then exit, the chilly suck of wet air the several fingers of sunlight the probing the licking and tickling her body calm and stark naked in the middle of all that clothing the way the clothing contained her the way the smoke drifted into and out of its folds. Thus touched, thus possessed, she was out of his reach.

10. And the fact that every cigarette displayed its own personality its own style its own set of idiosyncrasies such that lighting up was the initiation of a dialogue either dry or loquacious, fast, slow, intense, distracted, shy, dull, wily, or unpredictable. Some burned better on one side than the other, some clung to the ash and some dropped it, some ash made a tiny lit circular city, other ash coned up or faded to papery, silvery ghosts. Some blushed as she smoked them, stained themselves sepia colored, others stayed pure even down to the filter nothing more than a pale hint of what had passed through them. Some were bitter, some savory, none sweet or too terribly innocent but some more patient than others. Some were glorious to look at, some lost their shape. Some were soothing some scintillating some made her frankly physically nervous. All stank by the time she was finished with them. Regretful, ashamed, she was nostalgic for every last one and when her husband made his ultimatum *you must you mustn't statistically the children the thing already starting what is never it's immoral studies have shown* she dreamed of them nightly and woke with angry fierce desperate grievous yearning.

11. Did she hate him, then? No, of course she didn't.

12. Well, did she love him? Love? Her husband? Love is confusing love has too many postures too many objects too many permutations is what she answered her friend then sat for a moment in vague contemplation.

"We were married nineteen years."

"Yes," said her friend.

"Two beloved sweet wonderful rapscallion pain-in-the-you-know children."

"Yes."

"A boy, then a girl."

"Yes."

"The house, all those years, the car, the dishes to be done."

TWO STRAIGHT WOMEN TALKING

"Yes. Dishes."

"He didn't like dancing he didn't like snow he was frightened of sledding he wouldn't admit it he wasn't playful he didn't like music he wouldn't tolerate my music in the house in the kitchen when we were washing the dishes we washed the dishes together side by side in one sink."

"Yes."

"He never analyzed dreams he had no patience for speculation he never undressed me the way that I wanted but the sex was okay he knew my body inside out as you might expect after nineteen years."

"Well, not necessarily."

"He knew exactly what I wanted what I needed his tongue his hand his cock in all the places I wanted."

"Yes," said her friend.

"You know, he had a beautiful body."

"I know," said her friend.

"You know? And a beautiful cock."

"That I don't know."

"Not misshapen not out of alignment not bulbous not that scary deep purple not small not gigantic not with the vein too apparent but silky, luminescent—"

"How do you know so much about—"

"And with a freckle on the head, just off to one side, the sole part out of balance but who wants symmetry?"

"Not I," said her friend.

"Not me," she agreed.

13. **BUT THEN SHE SAT** remembering the water bed bucking underneath them the rhythm the sloshing the broad rectangular

storm of it and then herself her body her mind the calm in the eye of the storm of it.

"Calm?" asked her friend. "That doesn't sound right."

"Peaceful," she answered. "Serene. Untroubled."

"We're talking about during or after?"

"At rest. During."

"At rest?"

"Secure in the fact—"

"The fact?"

"That it would feel good. That it would bring me to climax. It always did. He was attentive patient watchful he never wanted to get there without me he never forgot me he never forgot I was the mother of his children he never imagined I was anyone else I was never embarrassed never worried never on edge hardly ever without proper birth control never not spent never not satisfied."

"Never not satisfied? Or never . . . what? Satisfied?"

"No tricks nothing ever unexpected no pain no biting no clawing no screaming no spit no teeth no bruising no scratching no begging no popped buttons jammed zippers lost panties."

"Oh," said her friend.

"He never lifted my leg by the ankle never wedged it behind his neck so he could thrust in deeper."

"No?" said her friend.

"He always made me come twice, one for me, one for him, sometimes hand sometimes mouth then the rest of him gentle and patient never half-broke my neck on the headboard never flipped me too far in any direction never dropped me off the bed never grunted never grinded never—"

TWO STRAIGHT WOMEN TALKING

"Never grunted?"

"Never did those gyrations, you know, that circular corkscrew grinding thing like the cock is a hand the way it grabs hold and pulls the way it—"

"How do you know?" asked her friend.

"Sorry?"

"If he never did it, then what do you know about it?"

"No backseats no secrets no fake names no lies no wrong numbers no stolen five minutes no sneaking no crouching no hats and sunglasses no grubby motels no friend's spare house no hallways no tumbling upstairs to the friend's spare bedroom no smoothing the bedspread no towel in the upstairs bathroom no mischief in the secret code of it the spying neighbors ignorant anyway of it the mailman delivering Christmas letters smack in the middle of it the telephone ringing the friend's mother chatting from Florida oblivious to it."

"Wait," said her friend. "Slow down. No towels in my bathroom?"

"No bathroom some days, not even a bed, no soft place for him to put his knees on no sand dune no dry leaves no untended grass just a tree to prop ourselves up on our heads in the moonlight not fifty yards away from the road and my husband driving the children back home on it the headlights sweeping the pavement but not the woods, not the trees, not I."

"Oh," said her friend. "So this is real. This happened. Why haven't you told me? You're not making this up! I have only one question. My mother? No towel in my bathroom? And who?" said her friend. "Who was it?"

"Except it wasn't me really it was somebody else. Some beautiful woman. Because, fucking, he always said, this other man, he always said, 'so beautiful so beautiful so beautiful,' over and over."

"Oh," said her friend.

"And 'so delicious so delicious so delicious.'"

"Oh."

"And then, if we had time afterward, talking, this other man, his hand in my vagina."

"Oh."

"Just there, inside, the way you'd rest a hand on a child's shoulder."

"Oh."

"The way you'd rest your hand on the head of a child to keep it still to keep it calm to keep it—"

"Stop," said her friend.

"A Dixie cup of wine in his free hand, the moonlight flickering, his face so unfamiliar so full of flickering shadows."

"Stop. Tell me. Is this true or isn't it? Real or invented? Because I know you invent, I know you like to imagine, to fantasize."

14. "THAT'S THE THING about the telephone," she said to her friend. "The way it seems to know everything the way it holds it in silence the way it watches the way it waits the way it sees, like a dog, the way it holds our transgressions tight in its own stupidity."

"Dogs aren't stupid," argued her friend.

"Telephones are. When there's no one to talk to. When he's gone when he's dead when I can't call him home from the office when I can't say come back there's enchiladas for din-

TWO STRAIGHT WOMEN TALKING

ner, it's stupid, yes, the telephone it's just a box just an object a lump no miracle."

"I'm sorry."

"I know. So that's where I sit, at night these nights when I try to smoke cigarettes next to the telephone I don't open the window to let out the smoke I don't sit in the dark I don't worry he'll drive up and catch me at it I don't think about him I don't strike the match for maybe ten, twelve minutes I just hold it in my hand and then when I strike it I can't stand the sight of the flame. The other night I tried something new. I went into the bedroom lit a candle poured wine stuck my hand in my own vagina and cried. No I didn't, that's a joke very funny ha-ha I don't know which I miss the most I miss them both they blend together the way they didn't before. My addictions. My vices. My husband gave me an ultimatum. Smoke another cigarette and this marriage is dead. I think he used the word *dead*. I think he said it then he did it. Very funny. Not really. To him, the smoking was an infidelity it hurt him that much so I stopped for two years but I never stopped wanting. When I was angry with him I used to fantasize his death used to fantasize sitting on his grave smoking five packs of cigarettes but now here we are and I can't light up. It's not possible it's not. Tell me it's a nightmare a fantasy tell me it's not happening."

15. THAT WAS TRUE about the telephone although she'd never thought of it that way before. The way it sat in her house knowing everything about her including what she needed that it couldn't provide. Lover. Husband. Cigarettes.

Courage. The phone was not patient, contented, or smug the way she sometimes pretended. No, it was a box of all the things that it couldn't deliver. After his death it didn't ring very often and when it did it was never him on the other end of it even though she picked it up fast so he couldn't get away. Dead, he was hopelessly fickle, wanting her but inaccessible. She couldn't hold that against him so instead she blamed the telephone or whoever else it dished up to her asking how was she as if she might say she was fine.

"Here," she would answer. "Just here."

Meaning, duh, on the phone.

Meaning, not dead not smoking not weeping.

Meaning, not listening to music, either, songs sounded like chanting too pressing too awful with need. "I have some wine," she might offer, sometimes an invitation, more often not. "I'm making tea I'm writing postcards I'm doing dishes laundry floors bath time bedtime lunchtime homework I'm thinking of mopping the walls." To her friend she exclaimed, "How could he not have known?" That the thing most denied is the thing more desired. One night she struck a match, held it up to her lips all set to inhale except the cigarette was missing she hadn't pulled it from the pack there was only the invisible presence of it "a philosophical moment" she said to her friend, "and you know what I did? I laughed. Out loud. And then I did something new."

"Yes?"

"Went down to the basement to the furnace to the pilot light and lit the cigarette that way, hand at the blue flame, head in a cobweb, bare feet on cement. One minute of that and then you wouldn't believe what happened I go upstairs the house reeking of tobacco the furnace venting some threads of it into the stairwell both kids in the kitchen dressed in their matching houndstooth pajamas, Angel and Angelica, Francisco and Maxine, I keep changing their names I believe that I gave them the wrong given names to begin with not to mention pajamas but both of them standing there shouting 'Who's smoking?! Who's smoking cigarettes?!' their hair a halo of curls overarching both heads. Two heads, two collars, six zippers, four footies, one halo."

"You're joking. Six zippers?" offered the friend.

"But the other part's true I swear it every bit of it except the part about the kids they're not mine they're too beautiful too wonderful they're some other better woman's."

16. ONCE, SHE WENT to an antiques store a curio shop a place of curiosities her three-year-old gleeful and proud in his stroller his bare legs crossed like an adult's his hands thrust in his belt loops on which he insisted so he could hook his fingers through them just like a man. There was a box in the window a narrow rectangular thing of tooled pewter just right for cigarettes if only she smoked them she had to take off her sunglasses in order to squint and see it. Inside was silk lining so tacky it might have been snipped from somebody's discarded cream-colored half-slip not worth half the money they wanted but she paid for the box anyway. The shopkeeper said, "My, what a beautiful child!" then stared perplexedly from mother to son and back again before adding, "His father must be *awfully* good-looking!"

"Sure, thanks," she said and tore the check from the ledger and years later has the canceled check still but not the box because she gave it away it was too empty looking too full of the things that she couldn't put in it not even the children's baby pictures fitted properly in it their too-adorable faces bulging and complaining if she tried to keep them in it not even their little balled-up toddler socks seemed comfortable in it not even their puffs of hair.

17. ANOTHER FACT ANOTHER HARD true palpable apparently immutable circumstance is that however much she wants she can't veer off the trail in the woods near the creek to make her way to the log on which she used to sit smoking.

18. FOR ONE THING her feet won't do it.
    For another the log is one of many all fallen all zigzag all turning to rot and sawdust so pleasant to lay the flat palm of a hand on and though she used to know her log exactly she no longer does she can't pick it out for certain she can't discern its dark hump from those on either dark side of it if she steps off the trail she doesn't know which hump to turn to which hump her body might recognize which hump might recognize her. In the past they had a certain camaraderie, her body and that log, her crotch to its cleft her thighs straddling precisely where they'd straddled before, the worn soles of her boots in their distinct proper places her fingertips stroking that rift in the bark that widened imperceptibly each time she stroked it. That's where she put the spent matches there in that rift until one day it seemed a violation an impurity so she tossed them instead into the creek. The creek made no sound no gurgle no chuckle no whisper a silence for which she felt profound admiration the children at home where they couldn't

find her didn't know where she was while her husband at the office gesticulating over his computer wasn't trying to explain to her his complex opinions on memos or books he had read or written when all she wanted were the vowels of her lover *so beautiful so delicious so delicious so delicious.*

19. "HE SPOKE IN A CERTAIN *way*," she told her friend, "he spoke in poetry in bed or wherever we were doing it he said, he asked, *in what position do you hold me in your heart?* the question a medley of syllables I used to hear while I smoked in the silence of the woods I can almost resurrect them."

"Almost," said her friend.

"And now I can't go back I'm afraid of that spot afraid of what I'll hear or not hear afraid of what I'll miss or not miss today I walked past it twenty-six times that damn log I couldn't let myself find it 'cause if I could I couldn't let myself sit on it."

"Okay," said her friend. "Like I almost believe what you're saying."

20. "BELIEVE ME," SHE SAID. "Except the part about the log except the part about the rift I never stuck the matches in it except the part about the creek except the part about the—"

"Stop," said her friend, the children stacking CDs on the dining room chairs the children stacking the chairs the children knocking over the CDs and the chairs. "Please. Just stop."

"Except the part about the squirrels except the part about the towel except the part about your bathroom except the part about the telephone except the part about moving away I'm not planning on moving not taking the children they have too many names I haven't already signed for the U-Haul believe me it's true except the part about desire except the part about the mint leaf except the part about the friend you're not my friend you're some other some better woman's."

BUT YOU'RE NOT

RIGHT IN THE MIDDLE of our evening at the minister's, I excused myself from the dinner table, followed a carpeted hallway decorated with framed photos of the minister, his wife, Serena, and a third tall figure wearing a double-breasted peacoat, locked the bathroom door behind me (there were two locks, one inside the knob and another that slid along a flimsy brass track), and then, after washing my hands, took off my dress and panties in front of the mirror. The minister wasn't our minister or even, hardly, a minister at all. Recently ordained, he served as a dean at the College of Arts and Sciences. He had no congregation and besides, we were atheists. My partner, Raye Yeet (no relation to the famous dead Scottish philosopher, she loved to confuse people by pointing out), had just been hired here in the math department at the university, and people kept inviting us over to dinner. Since

THE BELL AT THE END OF A ROPE

Raye was still freshly exhausted by the move, by the work of impressing her funny smart self on her new colleagues, and by the final, thinning trail of sleepless nights and zombie mornings caused by the spell of postpartum depression from which she seemed at long last to be reluctantly recovering, it was I who got all wound up about these dinners, for her sake more than mine. Raye longed to meet the people who would be our friends, people to go to farmers' markets with while spilling our secrets along the way, or, in the event we had no secrets, those of people who did . . . but it was in Raye's nature to be disappointed.

The wife's name, Serena, unsettled me for days—it sounded so full of promise, but even so I was dreading what Raye would find to say about her once dinner was over and we were on our way home. We would be crossing the frontage road, along an overpass approaching the flat gravel roof of a Walgreens store instead of passing into the tunnel of sycamore trees through which we used to drive home when we lived in St. Louis, and I would ask her if we had had a good time or not. I would know that this joke, meant to deflect Raye's discouraged response, wouldn't go over. In the sky above Walgreens, some stars would be visible in spite of headlights off the highway, but even as we glided past them, I would file the constellations away in my mind in a folder marked *It was okay, I guess.*

Raye would tilt her blonde head in fairness a moment, revealing the dusky throb of her pulse, a star blinking in the windshield beyond her ear as if to make up for the absence of earrings. "I guess I just didn't find her all that interesting," she would reply, and if the stoplight were red she would make a right turn instead of waiting for it to turn green again, underscoring the Yeetness of her remark. She would be driving because I didn't know how to drive a manual transmission, which was all we had since we'd sold my dented Saturn to avoid having to drive two cars all the way from St. Louis. The whole way to Wisconsin, Raye drove while I played in the backseat with Trace, picking up Rice Chex one after another, naming each latticed square of breakfast cereal after a famous person we hated, making the people beg for their lives, and then either sparing them at the last second or gobbling them up. Though it was getting to be time for me to find a new used car, I was putting off looking, just as I was postponing either looking for work or returning to school. I had paid our room and board all through Raye's long years in grad school by driving that rattletrap Saturn to work at the bakery, decorating cakes to resemble cloisonné boxes, and now that we were settling in, I thought I might just sit home with the baby for a couple of months, maybe even for years. I'd surprised myself coming to this greedy idea, but I didn't miss working. Aside from my car I missed nothing at all of our time in St. Louis; not the sycamore trees, not our lacy apartment six blocks from Delmar Avenue where Paul's Books used to be, not our great friend, David Karpakian, who lived with his canaries (free carbon-monoxide detectors, Raye joked) in the rooms below ours. Not the hits of cake flour I used to inhale when I opened the flour sacks there in the bakery, the edible silver dragees (free dental work, Raye said), the linen towels with the pictures of fat chefs dancing on them, my coworkers and our whisk-licking contests, spoon-juggling tournaments, or how we launched paper doilies off the countertop like motorcycles.

THE BELL AT THE END OF A ROPE

Nor did I miss Raye's pregnancy, the high, almost mystical way she carried it, her slender frame if anything rarefied by it.

Instead of missing these things, which had been so important to me while they were happening, I found myself inclined toward a yeasty domesticity I elected not to mention even to Raye. Now that her hormones appeared to be stabilizing, it seemed I'd earned the right to sink into some of my own.

LIKE I DID FOR ALL our dinner invitations, I baked one of my cloisonné cakes for dessert at the minister's. I didn't know yet that Serena was also a professor, or that she detested cooking. Except for my cake the whole dinner that night came directly from Sam's, the packaging in plain view on the otherwise untouched cutting-board island. I could see right away that my cake irked Serena. It made her feel put out. But I liked her anyway. Unlike Raye, I found all people interesting just because they were people, period. Even if we hadn't learned at dinner that night that the minister, whose name was Winston Lackwena, had "by a hair's bread-th" (you could hear the *d* when Serena pronounced it) escaped being murdered by Idi Amin some forty years earlier, I would have thought him interesting: because of the way he plucked five Nancy's Deli Spiral Tomato and Provolone Sandwiches off the appetizer plate and ate the stack in one bite while we were having our drinks; because of the rakish look of the narrow suspenders worn over his snug-fitting polo shirt (there was a weight machine in their bedroom where we'd laid our jackets); and because he kept the radio on, tuned to a high school football game. Winston had been a tennis player back in Uganda, Serena explained, not a pro or anything, just a member of a league, and one day he'd been warned by his ex–grade school teacher, who'd gone on to be a member of the disbanded parliament, that Winston's name was "on a list." His seatmate on the plane escaping Kampala was a girl whose toothache caused her to "behave improvidently," but when they got where they were going, Winston paid her dental bills. They'd now been married for three decades. Their grown twins, son and daughter, shared an efficiency in Cambridge, England. The twins "look exactly like Winston," Serena twice exclaimed. When they were first married, Serena didn't wish to have babies at all, but now that the twins were so far away, she regretted her earlier position as much as if she'd stuck by it and they had never been born.

"You don't know yet how lucky you are to be mothers," she said, bravely addressing Raye and me equally in this remark, when we were taking our seats at the table.

She was delicately built, with dark-black skin identical to Winston's, and wore a bright linen caftan with embroidered belled sleeves, not the best choice of clothing "if you were tossing and serving," she admitted while dressing the salad with Newman's Own. The minister smiled, just to hear her speak. She talked nonstop, maybe only tonight but maybe every night. Even after Raye and Winston eased themselves into the usual dissection of campus politics, Serena kept talking about cars and condominiums and how she didn't "know wines" and how she wished we had brought Trace with us instead of leaving him home with the sitter. I wished it too. I would have liked to watch him pull himself onto his toes via Winston's suspenders, and Serena, with her French-manicured thumbnail, halving a pimiento-stuffed olive, Trace's favorite bedtime snack . . . and I imagined her settling herself in the process, becoming more like her name, Serena, and less like a woman pretending to be at ease. As impossible as it seemed, I had never eaten dinner with a black person before, and Serena had never eaten dinner with a lesbian before, and somehow we both seemed to know this. True, I'd had encounters that were probably more important to me than they should have been, like at fourteen years old on the bus to my cousins' house in Kansas City, a man lifted my hand right out of my lap and predicted I'd never play keyboard. I'd been an idealistic teenager. I didn't like that I was white and that we lived on Lake View Drive where there really was a lake, which I was glad we couldn't see from any window in our house. It wasn't that I wished we were poor, exactly, or lived in one of the houses with no screens in the windows, which the bus drove by along the winding overpasses. Instead I wished, not in words but in a deeper and apparently pointless way, that there was nothing I needed to *be* at all. I didn't want to have money, not have money, or be the kind of person who lived with or without window treatments. I didn't even care to be male or female. I wanted to exist outside all categories and I would have been proud, had I known about it then, of the way I lived now, being a househusband even when I was having my periods. Raye seemed proud of this too, but mainly we just wheeled humbly along, like my favorite of Raye's elaborately framed posters of the shunya chakra, which hung on the landing in our little rented house, instead of half behind the file cabinet in her old grad-student cubicle, and which, aside from being the familiar graphical representation of the number *zero*, and which translated from the Sanskrit to mean *void-circle*, connoted the vastness of the firmament, including everything still uncreated and thus, paradoxically, eternal.

    Serena was a French Club, Russian Club, Swahili Club, Hebrew Club, German Club, and Portuguese Club member, we learned, not the kind of person to spend her Saturday mornings riffling through apple crates with other professors and their significant others. As if she'd spent too many hours in the language lab, she seemed to take solace in repeating herself, like with the thing about the twins looking just like Winston, and then reminding us again how "bless-ed" we were to be mothers. In the times she wasn't talking, she appeared to have some difficulty swallowing her food and also an interesting (to me) habit of pretending to saw very gently through the glass-topped dining room table with the blade of her butter knife.

Their bathroom mirror looked like their dining room table and, like the table, reflected a candle flame. A similar mirror once fell on top of me when I was a girl. I was perched on the counter at my cousins' house, watching one of my cousins depilate the fine black hairs, hairs I considered to be achingly beautiful, on her forearms. Her younger sister, now dead, was in the shower, shampooing her hair with an egg. The mirror came loose from the bathroom wall and flipped onto my head, not breaking. I was stunned but unhurt. With no exception I would always be stunned but unhurt by the things that might have hurt me, and despite a few setbacks it seemed like Trace was inheriting similar luck. Once, at Raye's mom's house, a sliding-glass bathtub door fell on Trace while I was preparing to run his bath. I had laid him on the mat, unsnapped his checkered onesie, and draped the onesie on a towel rod. I explained what I was doing every step of the way, not only in order to teach him words but to practice what I thought of as being truthful with him, as if I might otherwise tell him lies.

"I'm hanging your green onesie over the towel rod," I explained, as if I might otherwise say to him, "Your grandma loves to throw her sweaters out the window."

And I said, "I forgot to bring the oats but no oats are better than no bath," as if I might otherwise teach him that oats were extremely small chickens. He had chickenpox then, an angry, oozy case of hot, humid, summer-weather chickenpox that was making him miserable, so I was giving him a bath even though we had brought no Aveeno oats to be mixed with the lukewarm bath water. Raye's mom lived in Springfield, in the house Raye grew up in. Raye and her mom were downstairs in the kitchen "rounding up the bagels," as Raye liked to say. It would be peaceful upstairs in the gold-speckled bathroom, a justifiable retreat. I spread a terrycloth mat on the floor, laid the baby on top of it, tricked him into not getting up by singing "Eensy Weensy Spider," and slid open the speckled-glass bathtub door . . . which jogged off the track, struck the sharp, squared-off corner of the Formica countertop, and shattered into a hundred baby-size pieces that arranged themselves around and on top of Trace, who, thank God, was still wearing his diaper, though with the Velcro strips undone. A shard of glass as big as the diaper lay on top of the diaper. Confused, Trace waggled his fingers as if making the rain fall down on the spider, then screeched when I screeched, the two of us entirely losing control. Downstairs in the kitchen, up popped the toaster, releasing one bagel that had been sliced into four transparencies.

"Kat doesn't handle crises very well, does she?" Raye's mom asked when they were readying me and Trace to load us into the ambulance, the spinning light like a fan blade oddly visible against the noon air. As they shut the back doors, she stood adjusting the cape she had made of her sweater, not the sweater Raye and I had bought her but another of the eight sweaters, all cardigans, five of them red, that she'd been given at her sixtieth-birthday party. In a way it was good she was finally expressing her doubts about me, for it meant she accepted me as part of the family after ages of pretending not to know what on earth I was doing there.

"Kat handles things fine," Raye said, flexing her ankles. For Raye's graduation I had bought at a garage sale one of those beautiful maple lumbar-extender arches for lying on top of and stretching your back, which turned out to be something Raye must have wanted all her life without knowing it, since she purchased a second, portable model made of tubing and upholstery to be kept near the shuffleboard court on her mom's basement floor. Sometimes, after stretching her body along that arch, like someone prostrating herself in reverse, Raye really did look taller than before.

"Kat isn't a girl you'd want to have to depend on during an emergency," Raye's mom repeated, Raye dabbing at my cheeks with paper towel, as if reapplying a glaze of tears.

"That's why we love her so much," Raye answered.

Trace had only an inch-long head wound, the EMTs concluded. But he was covered in blood and so was I, the crust dark between my fingers, darker yet between my toes.

Raye escorted her mom to the hospital cafeteria. Trace and I read from a crate of Little Golden Books the whole time we needed to wait in a walled-off corner of the emergency room because, since none of the doctors or nurses on duty that day had ever had chickenpox, no one could safely attend to us. At last Trace was stitched up and a bandage like a ribbon of Civil War gauze was wrapped five times around his head, and he fell fitfully asleep. Only then did I scrub his dried blood from my toes, crying a little, all the fear I'd corked up. At the gift shop we bought a toy stethoscope, which Trace soon carried with him everywhere. He was a skinny, wan, bare-chested toddler with pocks on his face and that tatter of gauze, pulling his cherished stethoscope behind him like someone walking a tired kitten on the end of a short leash.

I KEPT OFF THE LIGHT in the minister's bathroom, preferring only the candle aflame in its jar. On top of a clothes hamper sat a phone that started ringing the second I sat on the toilet, and because I'd left the minister's number with our babysitter, hanging it prominently via the only magnet allowed on our refrigerator, I answered it.

"I guessed you'd be 'tossing and serving,'" said a person I just knew was the man in the peacoat in the photos in the hallway. He had an accent like the minister's. Serena didn't, somehow. "I didn't expect you would answer but I wanted to hear it ring. Are you miserable, Darkling? How have I reached you so easily? How are the plastic pineapples doing? Where is the telephone tonight that you reached it so soon?"

"On Serena's clothes hamper in Serena's bathroom here in Serena's condominium," I answered, amazed and disappointed to have learned, so quickly and by accident, Serena's biggest secret. The man hung up at once, as if not to have to learn about mine in return.

But that wasn't why I took off my clothes. Nor did Winston being a minister have anything to do with it, nor Serena's filmy nightgowns hanging on the shower rod looking like the curtains on the windows that had no screens. There was nothing even lustful about my finding myself in the nude in the mirror, since I had given up on lust when Raye fell off sex after the baby was born. I'd spilled food down the front of my dress, that's what started me off. This wasn't so uncommon; I often dropped whole forklifts of salads and things. I turned on the cold tap, took off the dress so I wouldn't get soaked, spread the cloth taut, and scrubbed at the stain with a bar of Serena's glycerin soap. After rinsing it clear I spread the dress on the counter and blew the cloth dry with Serena's hair dryer. I'd gone braless that night, which had to do, I think, with that private pool of hormones into which I was stepping ... and which caused me to take off my panties too. Conscious of my breathing, I started breathing in and out in the birthing-room way, to which Raye had not adhered. But I *had* adhered. And after six hours there came Trace's first cry, and Raye looking as if she'd lain there a decade but me wishing she'd spring up, brush her teeth, do her hair (two deliberately unmatched hair clips), grab her books and a coffee, and rush off to school, which was what she called work, so I could be alone with Trace. When Raye was asleep I picked him up and carried him between door and tray table, from 7UP cup to bed-control panel, around the visitor's chair along the room-divider curtain, explaining all these things as we passed them by. I promised him I'd tell him everything I knew about everything I knew about, which wasn't much, I admitted, although I promised to be smarter than the people on television, which was turned on but muted. "They're not really chasing each other around that couch. They're just pretending," I explained to the baby, who wore the funny little cap, like an ill-baked muffin, that the nurses had shown up with. Grateful to find that he really was paying attention to me, I resolved that it would be like that forever—me telling Trace things off the top of my head, nearly anything at all, just to form this bond between us that would be stronger than the bond that he had with Raye. Raye wouldn't have argued with this idea, I sincerely believed, which was exactly my point.

In the minister's bathroom, even while stepping out of my panties I paid attention to my face (I carefully met my own eyes, I mean, as opposed to skimming past them in the glass), by way of reaffirming what I knew about my body . . . that it was I, not Raye, who'd kept on the weight since Trace's birth. Also that my nipples were rounder than hers, like saucers, and of a stormier, more volatile hue. It was nearly five years since Raye and David Karpakian and I had first discussed the prospect of making a baby, during which all our deliberations had struck me as being so rational. For one thing, I'd be offered no maternity leave from my job at the bakery, while Raye seemed already determined to stretch out her dissertation writing for as long as was allowed. I couldn't stand milk, loathed spinach along with all other foods with folate in them, and as we all knew, I sometimes snuck cigarettes. Too, Raye had better carriage, and my feet were flat, so for a while, under David's steady eye (David, as our moderator, every so often brought out the hinged wooden case containing rows of English tea bags and bade us choose among them for the sake of ceremony) we debated the benefits of growing up in this day and age with floppy feet like mine, as opposed to exuberant arched ones like Raye's. And even though we were atheists, Raye wanted the baby born Jewish, in order for Israeli and perhaps even Polish citizenship (with all incumbent European Union perks) to be available to it.

"You're only a Jew if your *mother's* a Jew," Raye explained a little nastily to David, about which I gently chastised her later that evening when he was safe in his apartment feeding his birds.

"We'll hurt his feelings," I said. "He had no way of knowing a thing about that—about having to be the mother in order to be Jewish, or having to be Jewish in order to be the baby, or whatever it is, whatever you said," I added uncertainly, mucking things up on purpose in order to take the edge off my scolding. "He's a sensitive, ethical, unusual person. That's why we want him, remember, Raye?"

Raye said yes but that she wished we didn't need him. But David really was ideal. He had no wish to be a dad, although he wanted very much to be a progenitor. It was true he hardly cooed or clucked at the canaries, only freshened their water and swept out their old-fashioned cages, which he built and repaired himself out of redbud twigs, which now and then budded and sometimes bloomed.

Trace's birth was as easy as scooping the apple out of our weekly roast chicken, we all agreed.

THE BELL AT THE END OF A ROPE

Just a minute went by with me in front of the mirror, or maybe only twenty seconds. Before I'd left the dining room, Serena, Raye, Winston, and I had been talking of Trace and his doctor kit, which, aside from the stethoscope, wasn't really a toy but an assemblage of supplies—a handful of tongue depressors, some cotton swabs and rolls of gauze, a stack of pleated paper medicine cups, a needleless syringe, an old reflex mallet for tapping on the soles of Liza's feet, and a disposable pillow the exact texture of Bounce dryer sheets—given to us by the kindly doctor on that long, humid day in the emergency room. Liza was our babysitter, we confessed to our hosts as if confessing a crime. She was my surviving cousin's new husband's stepsister. We couldn't decide which was worse, we explained: that Liza was always late for babysitting, or that she showed up at all. She had, it appeared, pierced hair. There were hat pins in her hair, or else ornaments that looked like hat pins ("which I suppose we might refer to as hairpins," Raye said), stuck in every which way, with glittery raindrop-shaped beads on the ends, uncharacteristically fancy, for Liza was a sallow, taciturn girl in a dirty down jacket and gnawed-on gloves . . . but she had lovely eyes. Aside from being, in a manner of speaking, family, it was the eyes that saved us from giving up on her. Also, the minute she'd arrived in our living room that evening and counted out those nasty hat pins and stuck them in a cupboard, she'd kicked off her sneakers (no laces) so Trace could tap against her foot soles with his reflex mallet. She made her feet slowly levitate until he couldn't reach them any longer then tumbled backward off the ottoman, her stubby legs in the air. He didn't laugh at this trick as some babies might. Rather he regarded his patient with respectful solemnity, uncapping an empty Midol container and tipping it sideways above one of the pleated medicine cups. Her parents raised elk on a farm in Van Dyne, for meat and aphrodisiacs. It confounded me that Trace detected Liza's troubles, and that of all the adults he came into contact with, it was Liza he so tactfully chose to attend, Liza whose elbows he swabbed, whose ears he examined, and whose terrible grammar he kindly overlooked while pressing the stethoscope to her chest.

I put back on my clothes, thinking about, as I smoothed out the dress, Liza and her cigarettes, which weren't her cigarettes but mine, my awful Pall Malls. The weekly script went like this:

Raye: "*Liza* was smoking again! In the *garage!*"

Me: "*Good!* We don't want her smoking outside on the *deck*, in case she locks herself out again!"

There were only a handful of rules we had given our sitter. One: Conserve electricity. Two: No late-night horror movies in case the baby walks in in the middle of one. Three: No baths ("For him or me?" Liza earnestly inquired). No sweets before bed (they gave him bad dreams); a glass of milk *before* brushing, a book, and then the Weavers' recording of "The Lion Sleeps Tonight," which Trace adored even though it frightened him.

Without thinking I blew out the bathroom candle, unlocked the two locks, and went back into the hallway past the photos of the man in the peacoat, who had sounded sort of flu-ish over the phone. He was feeling sick of himself, I surmised, and he resented his self-pity, and he wanted Serena to hear this in his voice. The reason Serena kept saying the twins resembled Winston was that the other man was their father. He sent their birthday checks to Cambridge, avuncularly. Winston didn't know the truth of the matter. I wondered what it would be like not to know you weren't the father . . . except it wouldn't be like anything because you wouldn't ever know it.

Shortly I took my place at the table, where they were talking about Lake Victoria, which was the size of the Republic of Ireland, Raye said, but which in Serena's worst nightmares was shrinking to a puddle like the Aral Sea. Coincidentally, it started to pour outside, rain pounding on the skylights over the youthful cheers from the football game. Raye made as if to rise to begin clearing plates but Serena and I beat her to it while Winston removed the salmon platter, seeing how weary Raye was getting. My cake was carried to the table, where Serena declared she wouldn't cut into it. People declared this all the time, since the cakes really did look like cloisonné boxes, but then they did cut in.

Winston walked us to the car beneath a yellow umbrella, one at a time. Since I was first in the car, it meant sitting for a minute in the passenger seat as if on one end of a seesaw, the rain coalescing on the Rain-Xed windshield before sliding into the wiper trough.

Finally, on approaching the roof of the Walgreens store, when Raye said, as if in imitation of my finding all things interesting, "That's incredible they escaped being shot by Idi Amin," I told her I felt honored they had told us about it, it being such an important part of who they were and how they regarded themselves and each other. I didn't say a word about the man in the peacoat, because the thing with the mirror had made me need sex badly after all and I was pissed

Raye wouldn't. In a show of forbearance I cradled her hand on the gearshift knob, which was a dangerous gesture, she insisted, often throwing off my hand, only this time she didn't.

"Serena couldn't stand being at the table with us. Do you think it's because we're Jewish?" I asked, but since Raye was so intent on not dozing off while driving us home, she didn't get the joke.

"Trace is Jewish. I'm Jewish. You're *not* Jewish," she underscored, with a flinch of apology that made it clear she'd been keeping herself from saying this for quite some time. I didn't know where she was coming from right away, but soon I remembered David Karpakian feeding his canaries on the night Raye got sharp with him, the way he gently unlatched the doors of their cages and reached inside for the water bottles, being careful not to let something out that he shouldn't.

The light turned green and Raye drove through it in her safe, stern way, a raindrop winking at her earlobe, as if to make up for there being no stars. At home we found Liza sprawled on the couch, asleep like three sandbags. For two whole minutes, we went through our Waking of Liza routine, first standing over her calling her name, then prodding her arm, then in our stocking feet walking the trail of smooth oval yoga stones we'd collected off the beach at the lighthouse in Racine, massaging our feet while chanting her name, until at last Liza grunted and raised herself straight up into a seated position, Dracula style.

"Everything was fine? You and Trace get along really well as usual?" I asked while counting thirty-five dollars onto her palm and then bestowing on her all the Poppies Mini Cream Puffs that Serena had included in the take-home bag.

"Yeah?" Liza said, scratching at sleep. There was a Band-Aid on her eyebrow, of which she seemed unaware, one of Trace's zoo-themed ones, and she seemed to be waiting just like me for her to finish answering my question.

"Oh. I loaned somebody a flashlight," she recalled. "Their car was broke. Plus, they had to use the john."

"You what?" I asked.

Raye had gone up to bed, shutting off all extra lights as she passed by them.

There had been the stranger's car across the road with the hood propped open for proof, Liza said, so she'd led him to the kitchen where the flashlight was stored near the calcium chews, then showed him the way to the toilet. Now she tugged against her jacket zipper, hoping to unstick it. At last she dropped the jacket to the floor and stepped into the neck hole rather than rake the whole garment over those hat pins, which really were hat pins, not hairpins, I'd decided while she counted them out of the cupboard and stuck them back in her hair.

"They didn't have a umbrella," she concluded. At last she set across the lawn in the drumming rain.

In a daze I walked the floors of our little house, observing the things (the lumbar arch, a potpourri jar, the tour book of wigwams in Scotland) that might have been stolen by the stranded driver, and then at once, frantic, I rushed upstairs to find the baby on tiptoe in his crib, clearly ecstatic, singing "Wimoweh! Wimoweh! Wimoweh!" at the elephant mobile bouncing around. His eyes were wide open and he appeared to have been upright since before I arrived, grinning toothily at the place in which he knew I would appear.

"How was your night?" he might well have asked, he looked so smart and alert in his neatly zipped footies. I lifted him up, glimpsing through the doorway the shunya chakra. Trace's and my connection wasn't finished being made, but though it might not have a name, it was already catgut and forever sinew.

"Hard to say," I explained. "We made a half-decent showing and we ate a good meal. The blackened salmon was tasty even though it came frozen. Winston listened to football. I spilled half a plate of Ajinomoto Gourmet Premium Restaurant Quality Fried Rice down my front as usual. There were fake pineapples and a cola-smelling candle, and I looked at our life in their bathroom mirror. The flashlight's the only thing missing, my darling, and there are no secrets left."

2.

EDWINKA BRUNHILDE

On Saturday mornings, dressed in bleached jeans so snug they lift her up on the balls of her feet, her bottom like someone toying with a doorknob, her shoes as often off as on, her hair swept up in a drugstore comb, my mother spirits the telephone through the house while picking up scraps of disquietude advanced by the threatened shambles of the week. All receive her fond attention, her strict solicitude. The drapes unevenly pleated, the cups inching too close to the edge of the open shelving, the light from the skylights splintering purple inside them, she spirals like a maple seed from hallway to hallway, pausing only in her chat, the brief cusp of each exclamation oddly temperate, musing, a flat mote drifting about. The story she tells today is an old one; she tells it each time she makes a new friend. When my mother was barely twenty, a photographer teaching a seminar at her college asked her to sit. "Sit?" asks the friend. For a portrait, says my mother,

THE BELL AT THE END OF A ROPE

who arrived at the studio rain soaked, who fumbled in her bag for tissue and comb, and wanting not to disappoint, blotted even her eyelashes dry with a sleeve of her too-small childhood raincoat before depressing the bell. The doorbell made no sound. My mother laughs when she says this—a silent bell?—but the laughter fades out as she presses the dirty button again, her finger poised as she tells it, as if she might at this moment years later unpress it somehow, avoiding everything else that has happened since. But the door swung open, she was told to keep the coat on but loosen the sash, and directed to pose before a silvering mirror, looking slatternly. "Slatternly?" exclaims the friend, because my mother is not, was not, and won't ever be. The coat jerked her around but only like a treetop in a frowsy gust. After one roll of film, she was urged to remove it. By the drawstring hood she hung it on a coat stand. The stand toppled to one side but she managed to arrange everything upright again by carefully hanging her jeans on an opposite hook. In her sweater, panties, wool socks, and wet clogs, she was instructed to pick the papery spears off a spider plant while perched on a stepladder next to a window, the vinyl shade yanked halfway open, the pane smeary with soot and drizzle, her thighs clean as soap, the socks itchy around her ankles. Even now she remembers slipping one foot from its clog and reaching forward with her toe to rub a smudge from the window, the camera blinking at the gesture, the arch of her foot discernible even in wool, the clog tumbling off the rung of the ladder, the slack crotch of her moist cotton panties sprigged with bunches of tangled-up kites. In our house years later, even the closet containing washing machine, dryer, clothes iron, and measuring cup is glossy with mirrored Windexed surfaces, as is the inside of the pantry beyond. But what happened to the cans of creole chicken gumbo and the one of freestone peaches? And what became of the narrow flat box of honey straws kept there for tea, and why are two stacks of crackers gone from the box when last night just one had been eaten? My mother finds the only bagel left in the refrigerator. Also a clementine. She twists the round halves of the bagel apart, contemplates the clementine, and rolls the fruit under the palm of her hand on the counter to loosen the peel. Were she a different kind of person, had she been raised in a different era or place, she might have named her only daughter Edwinka Brunhilde, and this would be the enormous Edwinka Brunhilde's midday repast, the china plate obscured underneath it, the feast laid expectantly, eagerly, on the table, the butter knife upright in the marmalade jar since what on earth did Edwinka Brunhilde do with the mixed-berry cream cheese, the three-quarter stick of butter? The rainy day on which my mother sat for the photographer was a day the very opposite of this one, this one being awash in gold, and a funny, bright commotion happening just now in the vicinity of the leaf pile neatly raked behind the pool shed. Our dog, a retriever, strains against his lead in an attempt to reach the birds all congregated there, the squirrels busily neglecting the suet speared on the feeder in order to devour the things on the ground. My mother scrunches her nose while pressing close to the window to see what's so delicious—the peaches, maybe?—out there in the leaves. On her laundry rounds, she has come upon a scattered pair of slides, her favorites with the trapezoidal heel. Unencumbered by their narrowest of cross straps, the shoes are really nothing more than two miniature pedestals for her to clack back and forth on from window to window, trying to see what's so abundantly enticing to the wildlife today. The rear seam of her bleached jeans still holds the pigment; so do the crotch and an inky spot under the fly. The raucous birds are joined by an incoming flock, the dog lolls his hunger in my mother's direction when she eases a crack in the door. Peanut butter, dried apples, she guesses aloud to her friend on the phone. Snack spread, pumpernickel, since that's what was missing from the pantry this morning. For the third roll of film, she was asked to remove her panties, unbutton the sweater so that it opened around her belly and bra, then balance on the arm of a recliner while smoking a cigarette, although she wasn't a smoker and never will be. A wisp of smoke, drifting past my mother's face, was an ascendant ribbon of cloud, the nearest reach of turbulence. Her teacher, the photographer, who to each of my mother's friends' dismay turns out to have been an elderly lady in dangling earrings, squatted on her haunches but lost her grip on the camera, the lens swiveling sideways as if presenting to my mother the imperative to contemplate her future and its uncertainties. Maybe now was her chance to button up the yellow sweater and rescue the hems of her jeans from the photographer's pet rabbit and hurry on home to her student apartment, where in a sunroom of black-and-white tile the window seat was perfect for the reading of her psychology text, the book at rest on a pillow, open to a chapter featuring, of all things—my mother releases a forbearing sigh to the telephone receiver—appetite disorders, *you-know-what* nervosa, the young sufferers of which subsist on endorphins released by ongoing acts of self-deprivation. Starvation like a butter knife, a fluted china crock. Thieves, they are, emaciated smugglers of raspberry jelly, whole cheeses, and strips of beef jerky—plunk! into the goldfish pond where no one will crave a bite. If my mother were smart, she tells her friend, she'd fix a lock to the cupboards, the fridge. Ivy twined outside that long-ago sunroom, spider plants proliferated within, rain would slide along the pane if any still fell, my mother's hands straying from her psych book to a sheet of notebook paper to be creased, pressed, and folded in the shape of a flower. She clacks to the stairs, leaving her slides at the bottom but fitting right back into them when she returns, bearing another armload of her daughter's shapeless laundry. Why has that entire stack of flatbread, its wrapping torn down the middle, been placed on the flat roof outside the window of Edwinka Brunhilde's bedroom, where on a doctor's scale stand the talcum-powder ghosts of Edwinka Brunhilde's mighty feet, the calibration still hovering at eighty-nine pounds? Eighty-nine, she tells her friend. Yesterday it was ninety. My mother's beauty, as she stoops to pick up a train of bedsheet, and when she pauses at the table to help herself to a single wedge of clementine, and while hefting the tea kettle to see if it needs to be filled, is a thing of which she is always nearly, but never entirely, unaware. In that long-ago moment in the photographer's studio during which she had continued, even while removing her sweater and unhooking the bra, to contemplate her future, and finding that her beauty was not one of that future's uncertainties, she had resolved never to hold her beauty to blame for anything. It would be innocent of her, and of the things she asked of it. It would be neither accomplice nor alibi. It might be mistaken for boldness, vulnerability, mischief, self-confidence, expectation, demurral, and refusal, but such mistakes would never be its purpose, she would keep it like a blue plate, unmindful of its functions, its many conveniences. She pulls a cup from its place at the precarious edge of the shelf, to hold the steaming tea bag and spoon. As a grown young woman, before neglecting to turn away from the photographer's doorbell, she had never spent whole minutes unclothed in front of anyone before. Even there in the studio, the breathless lady photographer pretended not to be distracted by my mother's slender incandescence, pretended she might as well have been squatting to photograph the flank of a sand dune, pretended the shadowy, clefted places were no dewier than shadows and clefts of stone. The photographer is dead now, the camera a blunted, unconscious thing. The commotion surrounding the meal in the leaf pile behind our pool shed has slowed. Satiated, the birds heave themselves at the broad, flat rooftop, the dog still straining toward the steamed-up fare—honey straws and chicken drumsticks—they've left behind. My mother takes her place at the phone desk, pulls one foot from the trapezoid slide, and puts on an entirely different shoe found waiting there. For some time she will sit in two different styles of shoe, the elegant slide on one foot and an espadrille on the other, and be as if barefoot at the same time. Although the last of the rain had stopped plunking from the gutters when it was finally time to go home from the studio, my mother walked too quickly to enjoy the mild evening. She was eager for her homework chapter—the lank shirts favored by some anorexic patients, the anxious cinching of drawstring pants, the years of perfect family dinners—pass this, pass that—the mothers knocking their heads together trying to figure out why their daughters insist on regarding themselves as a Mac truck might, a truck unfairly saddled with truckishness. Starvation like a bowl, a lovely porcelain, hollow thing. Having refused the photographer's offer of money, still she wasn't distressed to have forgotten her raincoat and left it behind for the rabbit to nibble. Several months later she received a card of hand-pressed paper announcing the opening of the photography show. By then she had met her soon-to-be husband. She decided to attend the show alone, and tell him nothing about it. The pictures were hung in a coffee shop across the street from a florist's, and it was there among the plants that my mother collected her nerve, comparing features she had studied in another of her science classes—horticulture—to the examples she saw before her. Of all botany she prefers that least tampered with, she admits to her new friend on the telephone today as she has admitted to others before, the heavy waxy white stoicism of the snow lilies you stumble across in deep woods being far more persuasive than the fluty invented shapes on display in any nursery or garden. She examined the violets under their grow light, examined too her translucent knuckles under that glare, remembers the salty odor of warmed-up soil. Underneath her at the phone desk the swivel chair fusses right to left as she recollects crossing the road to the coffee shop and sallying inside. There she took a brisk, assessing glance around before deciding what actions and evasions might be required of a photographer's model, just as she does when she travels room to room in the house on Saturdays, the phone at her ear, a dust rag in hand, the rooms utterly heedless of her arrival, the cushions no more hankering to be plumped than the clock face to be polished. The threatened shambles of the week have never prevailed. Instead there is only this dreamy disarray, this pleasing inattentiveness of misaligned chairs, and nobody slouching or watching TV, nobody's gargantuan bloomers wadded up below the piano keys. Her fingers circle back to pause again at the clementine, pry off a second wedge and finally a third, tear a piece off the bagel, dot it with marmalade, and place it onto her tongue. How is it that the can opener lies spread-eagled outside on the grass, a can of everyone's preferred chowder upended where no one can see, maybe in the sand trap on the golf course on the opposite side of the fence? The new friend is having breakfast as well, both women at ease with their munching, slurping, and swallowing, the sifting of crumbs, the sticky tips of their fingers. While entering the coffee shop and glancing around at the clusters of gallery-goers, my mother was determined not to be shy, unnatural, vain, self-conscious, imperious, or overly modest. With humor and fortitude, she would respond to whatever flattery befell her. She would be upright, composed. She would be quietly, purposefully radiant, and always was, and always will be. If she were pregnant, as she suspected she was, and if the baby was a girl, she decided then and there, without saying a word to her soon-to-be husband, to name me, their daughter, Lark, for grace, ease, lightness, and an infeasible, paradoxical earthiness. None of the photos that the photographer had taken of my mother were included in the show. Instead the photos were of litter, detritus, filth, and garbage. A sheet of muddied, stepped-on newsprint blown against a lamppost. A snot rag clogging a basement window well. My mother dots the remaining quarter of the bagel with marmalade and then, considering, transfers the scraps of food from the plate to a paper napkin, so that it will look, she explains to her friend, "like it was left there by accident. That's the only way she'll eat it." She learned this trick from her textbook, she adds, placing the napkin casually next to the sink as if it were her own unfinished lunch. Starvation like a polished spoon, the blinking of Edwinka's insatiable eye. The friend will phone again later; my mother puts back on both of her slides, clacks to the car, puts on the driving clogs she keeps on the passenger seat, and starts off for the supermarket. By the time she returns home—to let in the dog, to pause at the yeasty stink of the yard, to take a vitamin pill, to scan the recipes for supper—both the left-behind mouthful of bagel and crescent of pried-open clementine will at last have been entirely consumed, the tea bag sucked dry, the napkin crushed into a tangle of stained, huddled petals holding in their creases traces of sweetness.

THE EMPIRICIST

DEE WAS CROUCHED on the shag carpet in Liz Danzig's bedroom making perfume with Liz when the telephone rang. Both girls glanced up from the row of paper cups into which they were stirring drifts of crushed rose petals from Liz's dad's garden. Every so often it was good to add a few drops of boiling water from the plug-in hot pot and let the petals steep awhile before resuming stirring. The water turned brown, not pink like the petals, and the bits of twirling sediment clung to the stirrers, which were really wooden spoons turned upside down. The smell was of rot. But if the handle of the spoon was dabbed against the insides of the girls' elbows, the smell of decay evaporated, leaving behind a watery smear that bore a faintly romantic aroma of wilted flowers. Encouraged, the girls pounded their spoons more fiercely. A little water on the carpet wouldn't matter, Dee knew, noting that Liz's water never overflowed the cup. Dee was nine and Liz eleven.

THE EMPIRICIST

Between them they were ten. When Dee turned ten, they'd be ten and a half, and soon, when Liz had her twelfth birthday, eleven. To be ten was ideal, since Dee felt grown-up, while Liz was excused from feeling the same. When the phone rang, Liz answered with the practiced aplomb of her dad's secretary, and pitched the receiver between her and Dee's ear so they both could hear.

"Yes!" She spoke as curtly as if the word were a command.

"Is this the lady of the house?"

"I'm afraid it's not," said Liz.

"Is this the *young* lady of the house?" asked the voice. It was a man's voice, velvety smooth. Amid the ruffles of the bedroom it was startling to hear.

It is. Dee felt the words before Liz spoke them.

"And may I ask how old you are?" the man inquired.

"To whom am I speaking?" asked Liz.

The man explained that he was a graduate student at C. W. Post College, performing research for his physiology thesis. Liz met Dee's eye and told him she was ten. Both girls had been driven many times past the C. W. Post College campus, farther west on Long Island, usually on their way with Mrs. Danzig to take Liz clothes shopping at the Miracle Mile. The heavily wooded road was studded with decorative hitching posts marking the split-rail fences of horse stables and riding schools. On the way home, Mrs. Danzig liked to stop at a farm stand, where the girls were instructed to select the reddest peppers, the least blemished tomatoes, and the freshest, firmest bunches of whatever came in bunches that day.

"I realize this might seem like a funny question but in the interests of science would you tell me what clothing you're wearing?" the man continued after Liz told him her name. Liz said she was wearing pedal pushers and a polo. Dee glanced at her own faded pink pants, grimy cotton undershirt, and the yellow sweater that kept being found no matter how many times she thought she had managed to lose it. A nosegay had once been attached to the undershirt but she had clipped it away with nail scissors and dropped it in a throat-lozenge tin where she kept some others.

"Polo. Good," said the caller. "And do the pants have an elastic waistband or a zipper?"

Both girls' pants had zippers in front. Liz's still had the snap but Dee's didn't.

"What style underpants are you most comfortable wearing, Liz?" the man inquired. His voice was warmer now, moister, like custard.

Liz said she liked bikinis in bright colors but that today's were white.

"And did you need to unzip to know what color they were or did you remember?"

"Remembered," said Liz.

Dee was impressed. She had needed to pull down her own zipper only to find that she was wearing the usual graying panties. The wooden spoons had been stood spoon-end down in the perfume cups by now, so as not to tip them over. Liz's bedroom curtains were always wide open during the day and dust motes swirled amid the handles of the spoons.

"Well, that's funny. I could have sworn I heard you opening your zipper," said the man.

"That was my friend, Dee," said Liz.

"And your friend Dee is sitting right there next to you," said the man. "And Dee is also eight."

"Ten," said Liz.

The man's silence lasted only a second or two. "Well then, that will make this all the more helpful," he said. "Two subjects at once is difficult to come by. How would you girls feel about answering just a few more questions?"

Liz gave her assent, but in a manner no longer quite so secretarial sounding as before. The man asked if either girl had ever touched herself between the legs.

"He means on purpose," Liz whispered.

Neither girl ever had.

"Why not?" asked the man.

"Just never did," said Liz. She made goggle eyes at Dee and stuck out her tongue.

"Good," said the caller. "Why not try it now, and tell me what it feels like, to the best of your abilities."

Liz shook her head no at Dee, but told the man okay. Loudly she rustled the bedclothes, aiming the telephone at the sound.

"Are you touching?" asked the man. "Did you find the soft round part? What does it feel like, girls?"

"I don't feel anything," she said.

"Nothing?" asked the man. He was deeply concerned. "Sometimes it takes a little while before you feel anything. Did your friend find the soft round part? Rub a little harder. Like a soft pink button? What's her name? Dee? What does it feel like? How does it feel?"

"She doesn't feel anything either," Liz said.

This went on a short while longer, the girls pretending, the man growing more disappointed. At last the man thanked them, saying that the girls had been extremely helpful anyway, and did they know the names and numbers of any other girls who might be interested in taking part in his research? Liz gave him the names of two girls from her class, but with the first and last names mixed up, and wrong phone numbers. She made her goggle eyes again once the man hung up.

"Creep," she said. "If he's in college, he'll fail."

She fetched a tray from the kitchen, lifted out the dripping spoons, and placed the cups on the tray. Already the waxen cups had begun collapsing. The girls would sell them door-to-door in the neighborhood, at a dollar per cup. They sold the first right away to Liz's mom, Mrs. Danzig, who was out in the backyard weeding. It was Mrs. Danzig who had chosen which of her husband's roses they might pick for the perfume-making venture—the aging red ones, she'd said, but none of the white and definitely not the persimmon. Her ordinarily sunburned shoulders were hidden these days beneath a crocheted blouse, but now that she was crouching in the garden it was possible to make out oblongs of skin. Dee poked a finger through a crocheted hole, but Mrs. Danzig never jumped at being touched by the motherless girl, the way some mothers did. She only reached into the pocket where she always kept a dollar. Liz slid the dollar under a rock she had placed on the tray, to be shared later on between her and Dee, and sent Dee to take the cup to Mrs. Danzig's bedroom and place it on the dresser amid the fancy glass bottles that showed in the mirror. Then the girls started up Lower Drive to Henry Kissinger's brother's house, passing Dee's on the way. Since Dee's dad would purchase all the leftover cups if there were any, it didn't make sense to sell to him until they'd finished with the neighborhood.

No one answered at the Kissingers', and at the house next to that, which was a castle house like the others, except for the Danzigs' red-cedar split-level, the driveway was padlocked. They sidled past the locked gate, climbed the broad grassy slope to the concrete wall, then followed the crumpling fortress to the entryway. The giant arched wooden door made it look like there were moats and crocodiles. But Liz and Dee had been there before and been greeted by two old men with a basket of Chunkies. Today only one man appeared at the threshold, his toes blue against the floor.

"Perfume," said the girls.

Liz added, "Cologne," lifting the tray so he could see the bits and pieces of rose petal dissolving in the cups.

"Such industrious children!" exclaimed the man, but in the end he only dug in his wallet a moment and came up with nothing, then limped back to the kitchen but came up with nothing again, and closed the door on one of the terrible hacking doubled-over coughing fits that could be heard through the windows. The girls circled around to the back of the house, where a gap in the wall opened onto one of the steeply terraced yards of the much smaller houses on Upper Drive. These ordinary houses were hit-or-miss. You never knew if a kid or a grown-up would answer the door, and then they wouldn't recognize you, or else it'd be a kid people hated at school. One house had a bright-red cobblestone driveway so recently painted that the WET PAINT sign was itself still wet. Across the grass ran four small dogs, two white and two black, that knocked the tray from Liz's hands. Both girls began to cry. A lady ran from the house brandishing a whip—four twined leashes, it turned out—and herded all four dogs into one yippy cage in the front hall closet. If all that remained of the spilled cups of perfume was poured together, there would be one cup. The lady led the girls into a yellow kitchen, where she gave them two twenty-dollar bills and eighty-one cents in change.

"Do you have a charm bracelet?" Liz asked.

"I used to," said the lady. Her wild hair was salt-and-pepper, her toenails were cracked, and the kitchen was too yellow. She dabbed some perfume on her wrist, sniffed, and dabbed on some more.

"My aunt's charm bracelet has a glass bottle with a folded-up dollar."

"Oh," said the lady. "Mine had a mink coat and a cruise ship, all the stuff we couldn't have. Also a Rolls-Royce, a maid, and a baby in a baby carriage." She clapped a hand to her mouth. "I can't even look at a box of animal crackers," she said.

"Give her my mom's dollar for change," Liz told Dee, who had rescued the dollar from the mess in the grass.

"Who says?" said Dee.

The lady smiled at the high trill of Dee's voice, the vigor of its delivery. Dee's scuffed sandals, her narrow build, the sudden combative set of her posture; each of these three qualities might have been predicted by looking at the other two of them.

"Would you girls like oatmeal?" the lady wanted to know.

"*Oatmeal?*" they answered.

THE EMPIRICIST

By the yellow kitchen clock, it was three when they finished eating their oatmeal, the caged dogs still yipping. The lady took a sip of the perfume by mistake as the girls stood to go, then poured the remainder into a glass on the window sill in which an avocado pit was suspended. Her avocados never took. Maybe this would work. The girls paused on the driveway, seeing footprints they'd made in the still-wet paint. Now that the perfume had all been sold, they didn't know which direction they ought to take. They might follow Cove Road to the dock at the Bay Club, or walk along it for a while in the other direction to watch Bobby Bates shoot baskets. Instead, they cut through the woods to get back to their street. In the woods was a waterfall without any water. It was one of their favorite places to go, but though to Dee it still looked like a waterfall, to Liz it was getting to be nothing but rocks with a box spring at the bottom. Wayne Smith's younger brother, Reptile, lay on the box spring, aiming a gun at his own face. Liz took one look, screamed, and ran. She dropped the tray in the woods, tripped over a downed log, and tore her pedal pushers. Dee didn't follow, and the gun wasn't fired.

The woods had a certain history, Dee knew. Things happened here that had no bearing anyplace else. A *Playboy* magazine had once been pulled out of a hole the size of a grave. A poodle later became trapped in the same hole and ran around barking in tight spirals until it was rescued by Jilly Solomon. Wayne Smith's switchblade was always a risk in these woods; you'd be walking along, and there Wayne would be, and there the knife would be. Last year a tanker truck of gasoline careened off Huntington Bay Road and crashed into the trees, resulting in some mothers not letting their kids in the woods anymore in case the supposedly spilled gasoline blew up. Jilly Solomon once set up a table in the woods for selling Chips Ahoy cookies and outgrown toys, but soon her hand-lettered signs were removed from the trees and Jilly was led door-to-door by her mother, in an attempt to buy back the toys. Kids who weren't supposed to eat candy snuck it in the woods. Exams and poor report cards showed up amid the brambles. Someone's mentally handicapped uncle once got lost in the woods, but for the most part adults never ventured there. Older kids smoked there. Bottles were found. Reptile Smith was just another weedy secret. Dee started off toward him down the steeply graded rocks, and took a seat on the box spring to wait him out. Each of Reptile's freckles was a perfect, infinitesimal rectangle. The gun was larger than his shoes, which he had laid on the box spring beside him.

"Here," said Reptile, holding out the gun in Dee's direction. Dee told him she wouldn't touch it for anything.

"How 'bout getting your mom back?" Reptile asked. "Would you touch it for that? It's not loaded," he added, aiming the gun at a place on the box spring between them, and jerking the trigger. The report knocked some dead leaves out of the trees. Reptile was pitched backward. A gaping black hole appeared in the box spring, and a slow ooze of smoke from among fragments of wire.

Late that night, because the fragrance of decaying roses had not quite vanished from inside Dee's elbows, she decided to skip her bath. She left her share of the money in the pocket of her pants, and climbed into bed in her underwear. Her bedroom window was open, her dad sitting outside on the cracked slate terrace where he'd been drinking his tea.

THE EMPIRICIST

After supper they'd taken their usual walk on the beach. The potato-farm workers had all gone home from their picnics, but their enormous fire pit still contained embers and discolored balls of aluminum foil.

"What did you do today?" Dee's dad had wondered, zipping his jacket against the chill.

"Made perfume at Liz's," said Dee in her high-pitched voice. "Liz's aunt has a glass bottle with a dollar in it on her charm bracelet, in case of emergency."

"She would," Dee's dad replied. "Did you lose your sweater?"

Dee realized that she had.

Now, in bed, she listened for her dad to scrape back his chair, the chair legs jagging on cracks in the terrace. Then she lay sleepily until her hand slipped under the stretched elastic of her underpants and found its way between her legs, where she discovered for the first time the soft round part. A car went by on Lower Drive, bumping along the potholes. As if to somebody sitting nearby in the room, she said, "It feels good."

REHEARSALS

Sylvi's mom liked to stop at Jeff's Seafood Shanty on the way to ballet, especially, it seemed, if the girls might otherwise get there on time. Sylvi wrinkled her nose at the smell, but Adrienne adored the sudsy docks and bloodied hose water, the seagulls wheeling at the boats amid feathery gusts of tide and gut. Jeff appeared to be several men at once, all wearing crisply triangular hats, and the clams clearly knew more than they let on.

Adrienne, in her pink dance slippers, tights, and leotard, a hoodie over her ponytail, walked the plank, feeling good to be small and in the middle of things. You had to be *real,* before you could be . . . what . . . *unreal?* she wondered, pausing near the door to greet the lobster in his sunglasses and Yankees cap. Then she and Sylvi helped carry the weighed, wrapped fish to the car, tiptoeing along past the slippery perfume of mollusks, of seaweed stewing where it clung to the piers.

By the time they reached class the girls smelled like two halves of an oyster—kelpish and pearly, secretive. The *powder room*, they were expected to call the dressing area, nothing but hooks on one wall of the foyer. Also, the *barre*, never the bar, even though here they all were on Long Island.

"Baaahhrr," Adrienne whispered in Sylvi's ear in order to provoke her. She had learned that it was easy to get Sylvi to do things—small, thoughtless cogs in a mindful wheel. Today's lumpy package of swordfish, for instance. All Adrienne had needed to do was slip the bag onto Sylvi's lap in the car, in order for Sylvi to carry it up the crumbling steps to ballet school, which was actually a house on a steep, wooded hillside, buttressed by timbers. The front porch was off bounds, and generally the pupils were expected to keep to the rear of the house, like balancing on a seesaw. In between was a bathroom featuring a scalloped black valance that turned out to be the shower rod draped with shrunken pairs of men's tights, and a drearily carpeted stairway leading up to a bedroom nobody got to see. The whole mess would be worth a fortune if it ever got out from under the Diehls and was properly resuscitated, Sylvi's mom, a county social worker, exclaimed on the way up the steps on the hillside, proud of not needing to catch her breath.

"Baaahhr, baaahhr," bleated Sylvi, loud enough to raise heads on the studio floor. Mr. Diehl scowled. Wearing yoga pants and slipper socks, he instructed the girls' beginning-level classmates while gesturing extravagantly at the other half of the studio, where the far more advanced company members were practicing extensions. Exactly as old as Adrienne's dad, he was at once more crude and more elegant, his long hair fashionably greasy, his fancy shirt cuffs unlinked. He promised to have no conscience, advertising this by not listing in the yellow pages (which meant he didn't pay taxes), and by requiring that you pay for each trimonthly session in cash in advance even while reserving the right to dismiss you.

"Dismiss them for what, though? On a whim? Or does it mean if they're not going to be Margot Fonteyn?" asked Sylvi's mom, leafing vaguely through the brochure guidelines as though she hadn't already critiqued them front to back. She clapped a hand to the side of her head, caught hold of her barrette, and clicked it decisively back into the frazzled prettiness of her hair.

"If they have poor disposition and get in the way, or if they're unteachable."

The reply came from the enormous Mrs. Diehl, in her armchair in the foyer, beside the bridge table on which sat the old-fashioned cash box and adding machine. Her dress, with its lumpy bodice and billowy sleeves, resembled a bed sheet and overstuffed pillows. She was too fat to climb the narrow stairs to the bedroom, so presumably she spent her nights in the chair.

Sylvi's mom didn't press the issue of any pupil being "unteachable." Instead she unfolded two wads of cash— a smaller wad for Sylvi and a larger wad given her by Adrienne's mother, since Mr. Diehl charged his pupils according to what he seemed to enjoy referring to as their *means*. Then she tactfully made a costume donation—some spools of broad, puckered ruching in a white plastic grocery sack—and in confusion took the droopy bag of swordfish from where it dangled off Sylvi's fingers and handed that over too. Mrs. Diehl lowered both bags fondly into the nearby costume footlocker, her eyes barely flickering as the girls filed past. It wasn't poor disposition that made Adrienne unteachable. Adrienne's problem was several things: poor turnout, complete absence of line, and just not looking as fresh and swanlike as the other ballerinas. She was too much a thinker, the crease sharp in her brow, and she wasn't allowed to shave her legs. She would have to wait until eighth grade. Her underarms she shaved without asking permission, using Sylvi's purple electric razor.

The poor turnout ruined Adrienne's frog kick too, or rather made her swim like an actual, injured frog, but this, like her clubfooted dancing, wasn't likely to pose an obstacle to the future that had been mapped out for her. According to her parents, Adrienne was to be a medical researcher. Even as a toddler she had passed whole hours hanging out in the hospital where they were doctors, pulling copies of the *New England Journal of Medicine* off the library shelves, and these days she was cultivating molds in her bedroom closet, with a kit they had been sent as a promotional item by a pharmaceutical company. The kit, which came in a box with a hologram of a sparkling apple on it, was supposed to have made her speechless with delight, but really it made her want to take a bite out of the apple, collapse on the closet floor, and not wake up for a hundred years.

Adrienne hung her hoodie on the hook next to Sylvi's, yanked up her tights, adjusted her slippers, and followed her friend to a place at the barre. She took ballet only because Sylvi did and, like Sylvi, because of Sylvi's second cousin, Francine, who was one of four principal dancers in Mr. Diehl's small, local company, which had once been written up in the

New York Times. Recently Francine had auditioned for the Joffrey, and now she and Mr. Diehl were waiting to learn if she had gotten in. At fifteen, Francine was the jewel of the school, the achievement that saved Mr. Diehl from having to put on more airs than he already did.

"In a way," he had read aloud from his letter to the Joffrey, "I hope that you don't accept Francine and take her away from our critically acclaimed little company. But in another way, of course," he added, "I want her to have this opportunity for which we've worked so hard over so many years, even though her family is of limited means."

Onstage with Mr. Diehl's company, Francine was paired with Jackie, whose tights were on the shower rod. The tights only looked shrunken until he put them on. In Sylvi and Adrienne's eyes, Jackie's girlish name only amplified his masculine appeal, his embarrassing sensuality. He smelled of sleeveless undershirts, the tufts of hair stiffening under his arms. Did he eat enough? they worried. It was hard to tell; he was so good to look at, such a triangle, and with that floppy mop of hair. There was that thing he did onstage that made the audience swoon—balanced himself against a beam of light, and then deliberately, *flop,* the hair fell forward, upending the symmetry. Online, before bedtime, Sylvi and Adrienne held long, sleepy conversations, encouraged by the things that Francine occasionally confided in them about Jackie. Francine was in the know because she was in the company and knew all sorts of things that went on at the Diehls', like when Jackie was doing one of his crazed, fierce, meditative solos back and forth across the studio and his tights split wide open straight down the middle but he kept on twirling.

Or like the fact that, being not yet seventeen, he had lied about his age—saying he was nineteen—to get his job in New York City, driving a millionaire's limousine. According to Francine he made good tips, but all of it got written up in Mrs. Diehl's ledger and vanished into her cash box, for room and board. Years ago Jackie had run away from New Jersey because his parents forbade him to dance, but the official, public story was that he was Mr. Diehl's nephew who would take over directorship of the school when Mr. Diehl gave up teaching and Mrs. Diehl wearied of keeping the books, or more likely died, since on top of weighing three hundred pounds she smoked constantly during the rare times she managed to get out of the house.

Adrienne believed that what Jackie really wanted was to escape Long Island, leaving the Diehls forever behind. How she knew this she couldn't say, but she longed to help him make it happen, for she could tell he was unhappy under the skin. He looked distressed, like fabric. Unexpectedly the young man had taken a liking to her. Recently he had started calling her *Adie,* and showing a vivid mixture of sympathy and envy, he would ask what it was like to be the daughter of two doctors who expected her to become a medical researcher. Sometimes, exposing to her the nape of his neck, he asked for her help in fastening or unfastening his necklace, which had once been Mrs. Diehl's. There wasn't a pendant, only the chain with a faulty clasp and an appearance of painstaking devotion about it, as if spun link by link by a jeweler spider.

Later that same week, the fog was so thick that the girls climbed all the way up the hillside to the wrong house, one with a freshly painted threshold. Sylvi was all for crossing this bright new threshold and pretending to think they were in the usual shabby place—two girls in plastic rain ponchos pushing the furniture out of the way in the stranger's living room.

But the door was locked, and then, oddly, once they'd climbed back down to the Diehls' house, they found that the Diehls' door was locked as well. By now they were only twenty minutes early for class. Adrienne's mother had driven them that day and needed to drop them off early in order to arrive on schedule at the operating room. She was an anesthesiologist. Adrienne's father was the surgeon, so the joke at cocktail parties was that she knocked you out so he could slice you open.

The girls knocked and rang the bell, the top of which came off on Sylvi's fingertip, a full moon deprived of its plastic glow. She flicked it into the fog. For a minute the girls wafted above the nonview of the harbor, the masts' muffled clanging encircling them, the fog dripping down their necks, clinging to their skin.

"I feel like a waif," Adrienne said, watching a runnel take on speed in a fold of her poncho.

"You look like one," Sylvi confirmed. "What's a waif, anyway?"

"Someone with goose bumps," Adrienne explained, and then said to herself, *someone who spends years combing through medical journals in the hospital library looking for pictures of naked patients with large black rectangles covering their eyes.*

Just then the door was opened by the other principal ballerina, the one who looked like Gwyneth Paltrow. She gave them an insipid, teary-eyed look and let them inside, where everything was just a little off-kilter.

That is, although most everything was in its usual place—Mrs. Diehl at her adding machine, the company crouched in the dressing area, making ribbon and seam repairs to their worn-out shoes and costumes—the atmosphere felt depleted somehow. Something smelled bad. No music was playing, and Mr. Diehl sat drinking tea at the piano bench in the studio. There wasn't a piano, but still you didn't drink tea in the studio, you drank it standing in the foyer.

"Who died?" Sylvi shouted, to which everyone all at once offered the news: Francine had been accepted at the Joffrey School. She'd received not a letter but a phone call "from Arpino himself." She would be saying good-bye. They wouldn't see her anymore, except for Christmas holidays or maybe only once a decade to say hello and see how things were going.

"Shhh," cautioned Jackie, with a flick of his eyelashes in Mr. Diehl's direction, and then, speaking in a fake British accent, "Ostrich feather, darlings?"

He handed Adrienne not a feather, of course, but one of the heavy lead paving bricks he sometimes carried around in practice for having to lift ballerinas. Braced for the weight of it, Adrienne passed the brick along to Sylvi, for Sylvi was better at this than she was—making solid lead look like something airy and light. Indeed the brick appeared to flutter aloft as Sylvi carried it across the wood floor of the studio. She had natural line and flawless turnout, but more than being agile, Sylvi wished to be feared. "Filigree, dear?" she asked, and passed the brick to Francine, who had her mind on the Joffrey so didn't take note of the fake British accent. Later it would seem that there should have been a lull in the already listless atmosphere of the house, a stalled second telling you that the mood was about to flip. But there was no such lull, for Francine dropped the heavy brick right away, and everything else was entirely, immediately forgotten. There was a horrible scream, the black slipper crushed and bloodied, everyone rushing forward to see. Even Mrs. Diehl climbed out of her chair, smudging the walls with her fingerprints. Mr. Diehl shouted to clear the way. Some of the girls were crying, and one threw up. The four o'clocks started arriving for class, but were told to come back next week. Jackie fled upstairs, and Sylvi was nowhere to be seen, but Adrienne could think of no reason herself to hide, generally going unnoticed anyway. The second male dancer carried the screaming Francine down the hill to his car, and rushed her to the emergency room.

Near five o'clock, when on a normal day class would just be ending, it was Sylvi's mom who at last found Sylvi. She was all curled up on the damp front porch, where you absolutely weren't supposed to be because the joists that secured it to the front of the Diehls' house were rotted through. The window screens were shredded, and the floor slanted perilously over the fog. Miles away a ship's horn sounded. The dead leaves on the porch were eons old. Sylvi lay in a corner too far away to be reached from the doorway, and no one dared step onto the wobbly slats to reach her. Instead they resorted to lies, hoping to persuade her to shimmy back on her own. Francine's foot would soon be as good as new, they claimed, and the dent in the studio flooring was where the subfloor needed fixing anyway.

Mr. Diehl, who until this moment had been keeping himself pale and resolute, trying to take stock of one disaster at a time, finally gave in to his temper. He took hold of Adrienne's arm and flung her onto the broken porch slats, where she grabbed the stretchy neckline of Sylvi's leotard.

"Now get them out of here already," he snarled at Sylvi's mom, yanking both girls to safety just as the porch lost its grip on the house and swung several notches lower, coming to rest amid the crowns of some trees.

"THE NECKLACE *used to be* Mrs. Diehl's since their first year of marriage but now it belongs to Jackie," Adrienne was telling Sylvi a week or two later at Jeff's Seafood Shanty, from where they would be driven to the public library to listen to foreign-language tapes in the audiovisual room instead of going to ballet school, which Sylvi's mom was boycotting for the time being after the episode on the porch.

"Mr. Diehl gave Jackie Mrs. Diehl's wedding necklace," Sylvi explained at once to her mom.

A gloved handful of glistening scallops was dropped on white paper, the needle quivering on the scale. Scallops didn't look like whole animals; you could see nothing about them that kept them alive. Later that day, Sylvi's mom would need to appear before a judge to testify in a child-custody hearing, so she wore her courtroom clothing—a pencil skirt and heels. Her hair was its usual midday wreck, the barrette lopsided among the tendrils.

"One thing I'd like to know," Sylvi's mom said, "is was he always named Jackie or is that only what they call him at the Diehls'? It's quite a name for a boy."

"He's not really their nephew, you know. And when he moved in he was, like, thirteen," Sylvi went on. "He doesn't have to go to school. Nobody knows he doesn't because he practically never did."

"Not even his parents. They don't have a clue what's going on with him," Adrienne said, accepting the neat, wrapped package of scallops, along with a box of Carr's Water Crackers.

"Jackie says it's violent. Ballet," Adrienne added when they were back in the car, the cracker box open, the crackers spilling between her and Sylvi. Ever since she had driven forward one time without thinking, practically skidding into the water, Sylvi's mom always took a moment to collect herself before backing away from her dockside parking place, but today she seemed even more flummoxed than usual.

"Ballet is *what? Violet?* Not even his parents *what?*" she asked.

Adrienne leaned her head in patience against the car window. It was the *spectacle* of ballet, the *artifice* that was violent, Jackie had explained. There was the stage, the curtain parting, the big, conscious glow on the rosined wood. It was awful. It was too good to be real. It didn't exist, but it made you really, really want to go there.

"Violet. I can see that," Sylvi's mom went on, nearly losing her hold on the steering wheel in order to jot something onto her clipboard. "Jackie's hurting, isn't he? I mean, he doesn't like to show it but you can see it in his eyes, can't you, Adrienne? He was thirteen when Mr. Diehl gave him the necklace, Adrienne? His parents don't know where he is?"

EVENTUALLY, TO MAKE UP to Sylvi's mom for what had happened on the porch, and so as not to lose two paying pupils, Mr. Diehl invited both girls on the annual company excursion to New York City, for which the *program,* as Mr. Diehl called it, included observing the prestigious New Village Ballet at their master class (the director and Mr. Diehl had once performed in another company together), and then lunch at this year's affordable stand-in for the Russian Tea Room.

On the day of the excursion, Francine had bravely wound her hair in a leather belt, cinching it into a spongy topknot, and wore a vintage crepe dress of a creamy color that, crutches notwithstanding, showed off her strong, cylindrical carriage. Her foot was healing better than expected, and though it would certainly never regain the strength required for her to study with the Joffrey, she would likely be ready for Mr. Diehl's *Soiree in the Park* series this summer, as long as she didn't have to go on toe.

Sylvi wore a sequined camisole and a denim miniskirt. The men were in black jeans, while the corps de ballet girls wore angular heels and bias-cut blouses. All the girls carried small evening purses on slender straps, and even Mrs. Diehl looked less like an unmade bed than usual.

"You're going like that?" Sylvi scolded once they were filing onto the train.

Mr. Diehl groaned. "Don't tell me," he said.

Adrienne had on baggy corduroy pants and a brown thermal henley T-shirt with one missing button. Plus, she had forgotten to bring her purse.

"Two doctors send their daughter to New York City with no money!" he exclaimed.

"I have my credit card," said Adrienne.

Mr. Diehl emitted a burst of laughter. Jackie offered Adrienne the seat next to his but one of the corps girls got to it first, so Adrienne chose the bench facing Jackie's, which meant she'd be riding backward.

"What's that?" someone asked.

"It's my journal," said Adrienne.

"Then why don't you write in it?"

"I forgot my pencil. It's in my purse."

A man lurched down the aisle as the train pulled out of the station. Sylvi plucked a pen from the man's back pocket and dropped it in Adrienne's lap near the journal, which had a slightly metallic, marbleized cover held firmly closed by an attached loop of stretchy black ribbon. The pages were ever so faintly lined. She had bought it one day in the hospital gift shop while waiting for her parents to finish up in the operating room, and it remained her most treasured possession.

"What does she write in it?" the dancer sitting next to Jackie asked.

"Whatever comes into her head," Sylvi said proudly.

"Whatever *does* come into her head?" joked Mrs. Diehl. It had been a huge production getting her on the train, but now that she was seated she was in a better mood, uncapping her water bottle and arranging her creases and folds.

Adrienne flipped open the journal to the last entry, a short story in the form of a letter she was writing to her mother.

To Dr. Roberta Altschuler or Current Resident at 47 Bread and Butter Lane, the letter began. She had started it the night before and now picked up where she had left off, inspired by the replacement of pen for pencil and by the swaying of the train, which caused the pen to seem to write on its own. Left to her own devices she always used pencil, because lead lasted longer than ink—in vaults, in archives, across manuscripts and documents. Ink faded, paper deteriorated, but pencil lead clung as if to particles of air.

"To Dr. Roberta Altschuler or Current Resident at 47 Bread and Butter Lane, Northport, New York," Sylvi recited aloud as Adrienne wrote.

"My daughter and me we were gests at your address at Mr. Gerald Po's party, who lived there before you moved in. We slep in the gest room at the end of the hall" (this was Adrienne's room now, Sylvi paused in her reading to explain) "because my car was total and no hotel was where anyone was driving pass on their way home. I would say it was a dark and stormy night accept it wasn't. I'm a man, not a woman. My wife was in Washington, the state. My daughter, Adrienne, was ten. It was her birthday but the party was to celebrate Gerald Po's divorce. May 22. But it was a warm night, not hot but lukewarm, and since it wasn't apt for her and me to sleep in the same bed, I slep on the couch in the sewing room in my clothes. In the middle of the night I hear sounds but then I think it's only some other gest in the kitchen, since they were smoking in there. Nobody quit smoking then, since it was practically sixty and a half years ago but I still don't like the smell. So I fell back asleep. But Adrienne wasn't in the gest room in the morning and the bed had not been slep in, it was totally made. My little girl was disappear."

"Awesome!" exclaimed Sylvi.

"Who's Dr. Roberta Altschuler?" someone asked.

"Adrienne's mother. And that's Adrienne's birthday, May 22."

"It's running out of ink," somebody warned from over Adrienne's shoulder.

Someone else whisked the pen from Adrienne's hand—the pen seemed to jump out all on its own—and everyone scrambled around for a new one. An eyeliner pencil, someone asked?

"No. It's a man," said Sylvi, batting her eyes at Jackie, who was known for dramatic eyeliner use on nights he performed at *Soiree in the Park,* and on the smudged mornings after. Moths flitted darkly about the stage, and there would be Jackie's eyes, like tropical butterfly wings: emerald, glitter, indigo.

"Here's one," someone offered, the same pen Adrienne had just been using.

Even though it was a pen and not a pencil, just to hold it in her hand again and let the nub hover over the paper created a steamy, charged climate that exerted, Adrienne decided, both a violet *and* a violent hold on her. You wanted to just shake yourself up to get your blood flowing and rematerialize in a different place and time, like on a bed of cool grass beneath a darkening sky.

"Why does she hold the paper so close to her face?"

"Because she's blind," answered Sylvi.

We've never saw our beloved Adrienne again, Adrienne wrote. She paused for a moment, nurturing a curious affection for her imaginary letter writer. His forthright misspellings, his hopefulness in the face of an apparently hopeless situation, the idea that he had waited sixty years to ask for help, stirred her as if he were sitting beside her, watching time roll past the windows of the train.

REHEARSALS

Here's what Adrienne looked like, the ink skipping a little as she went on writing, *even though she would be old now to. But what we mean is maybe our daughter got trapped in your gest room closet, not dead we mean but in another world and nobody hardly opens it.*

"Who's good at drawing?" Adrienne asked.

The train had already stopped in Cold Spring Harbor and Syosset and was heading for Hicksville.

"Cindy draws," said Jackie.

Cindy was the unlikely name of Mrs. Diehl.

The train swung sideways just as Mrs. Diehl was handed the pen and the journal. It was true, she could draw. The likeness was acute, especially the furrow between the eyebrows. On consideration, Mrs. Diehl added the pimple that had shown up on Adrienne's chin that morning, like dotting an *i*.

"Make her look really happy," Adrienne encouraged, but Mrs. Diehl handed the impassive face back across the aisle and turned her attention out the window onto Great Neck, where she had grown up.

"Change trains in Jamaica!" Francine turned around in her seat to call. She and Mr. Diehl had been sitting all this time some benches away, talking only between themselves. Together, the backs of their heads looked exiled and intimate, her topknot atilt above his comb-lined hair.

With a swishing of skirts, everyone gathered their elegant things. Adrienne carefully closed her book, looping the black elastic ribbon securely around the binding and giving it a final *snap*, like locking a trunk with a special key. Then she hitched up her corduroys to keep from scouring the floor with their hems.

THE BELL AT THE END OF A ROPE

AFTER THE TRAIN ARRIVED at Penn Station, the group found itself being shepherded into and out of buses, and steered from street corner to street corner. Finally they were ushered up some stairs to a doorway leading into a vaulted studio, where Mr. Diehl commanded them to take off their shoes before filing inside to a row of folding canvas director's chairs on a low black spray-painted platform. Though the fog had been thick on Long Island for weeks, the streets of New York were full of sunlight, which reached the studio through a trio of skylights to cast angular motes in the room. A troupe of dancers in athletic gear stretched at the barre or thumped purposefully around in preparation for warm-up, flexing their big feet and clearing the floor of Pilates balls and fitness mats. Finally out stepped Mr. Diehl's friend, the famous director, and the New Village dancers arranged their lithe, gleaming postures before the mirror, the dust motes quaking, the director percussing, his crotch unsparingly outlined in shiny leggings.

At the sight of such telltale contours, Adrienne nudged Sylvi with her elbow, at which Sylvi yelped and flung herself deliriously too far sideways, her chair collapsing into Adrienne's. Both girls tumbled noisily off the platform, knocking over a trio of bongo drums. The master class was halted before it began. Mr. Diehl sat bolt upright, mortified. The dancers stood as dancers do, duck footed, hands on hips, cruelly regarding their audience.

Naturally, once order was restored and the master class was finally, respectfully, over, and Mr. Diehl and his charges were slinking off to the restaurant to eat, it was Jackie who bore the brunt of the collective evil eye. Sylvi and Adrienne were Jackie's fault, Mr. Diehl accused. If not for Jackie and his *cobblestone,* he exclaimed, they would never have been invited to come on this trip. Angrily, Mr. Diehl took a fierce lead on the sidewalk, the loyal Francine on her crutches at his side. Jackie and Sylvi fell behind, Adrienne catching up in her sneakers, which rattled because some pebbles were trapped in the soles.

"I have to tell you something later about Sylvi's mom," she confided to Jackie, keeping her eye on the broken-up spaces between the buildings, the funny things people chained to their fire escapes.

There came a honk from the side of the road, where Mrs. Diehl had been following along in a slow-moving cab. It was the same cab that Mr. Diehl had negotiated for her at Penn Station when everyone else took buses, and that had driven her to the New Village Ballet studio and parked the whole time with the meter running so she could sit in it and smoke. A whole pack she had gone through, and now she sent the ill-favored Jackie around the corner to buy her two more packs and a fresh lighter, so he was gone when they found the restaurant and had taken their seats at three pushed-together tables covered with threadbare linen. The wallpaper was flocked, the menu Eastern European, and the people at two other tables stood up to go just as Jackie appeared outside the window, heading for Mrs. Diehl in her cab. He wasn't walking; he was crawling along on bent elbows and knees, the two packs of cigarettes resisting all his showy, balletic efforts to drag their pretend weight across the street, where luckily there weren't any other cars.

Adrienne ordered a soup with dumplings, which tasted like white bread when you had chewed it into balls. Anastasia Volochkova had been fired from the Bolshoi for weighing all of 109 pounds, so everyone else only picked at their food. At the end of the meal, people slid their cash onto the table like bets at a card game.

"You'd look older with your hair up," Jackie told Adrienne. Disheveled by his act outside on the pavement, the white shirt filthy, his chest hair dusty as if with talc, he had taken the only seat left, the one Adrienne and Sylvi had saved between them, and now he was winding Adrienne's hair around the pen from the train, trying to tame down the frizz. "But you probably don't care so much about what people think, do you? You should keep being that way, Adie. Only don't call attention to it. Not that you would. What was it you wanted to tell me about Sylvi's mom?"

"Nothing," whispered Adrienne.

"What?" piped Sylvi.

"Let Sylvi tell you," Adrienne said. "She can tell you on the train. About your mom's *clipboard*," she emphasized to Sylvi.

"At your convenience, Adrienne," Mr. Diehl spoke from his end of the table, waiting for her to contribute some money toward lunch. He squared his shoulders, showing off for all the people who paused at a newspaper dispenser outside the window. All the terrible news in the world didn't stop people from spying on other people in restaurants, checking out what they were eating and how impressive they were. To see people peering through the window at all the ballerina hairdos and bias-cut blouses awakened one of Adrienne's complicated thoughts. It had to do with sharks not knowing a thing about dry land—not knowing that houses and streets and poems and stories and salad bowls and nuclear power plants and leukemia even existed. She thought of her injured version of the frog kick and of a shark following along not knowing that she was the daughter of two doctors and was growing penicillin in her bedroom closet. What she wondered was whether the shark's being totally ignorant of everything in the world made the shark more, or less, important than people.

She reached into her pocket, laid her credit card on the table, and scooped up all the cash that everyone else had put there. She had watched her dad do this. She flattened the bills, unlooped the elastic ribbon from around her journal, and though it gave her a terrible pang to do so, slid the ordinary currency between the pages of her story.

"Leave a tip," one of the dancers advised, and showed her how to complete the tip line on the credit card slip. Her own signature was unfamiliar to her on the flimsy slip of paper, more grown-up and less philosophical than when she wrote it in her journal.

IT WOULD BE DARK on the train on the long way home, dark enough that Adrienne wouldn't be able to see outside. She knew she'd see only her face in the glass, and that she'd think of Sylvi's mom in a fitted blazer, knocking the next day at the unmarked door of the Diehls' house. Sylvi's mom would be holding the clipboard with Jackie's name on it, and would be leading some people from Child Welfare, having waited until after the excursion to New York City to do what she felt she needed to do.

Adrienne thought of how the news would play it—the single, cluttered bedroom at the ballet school, the footlocker of costumes stinking with fish, the students pulled from the barre, Francine's ruined foot, and Jackie being hand delivered to his parents in New Jersey, where maybe all the cousins resembled him, but not anywhere near as beautiful.

Here's how he walked down the steps at Penn Station: gliding like a cable car and glancing around as if at a view of the slopes. On the train he sat with Sylvi, Adrienne staying just close enough to be able to hear what Sylvi told him. At Jamaica she watched Jackie boarding the new train like everyone else but then ducking out the door on the opposite side of the car and hurrying away on the platform, past the poster displays and the garbage cans, slowing his pace only once the roaring on the tracks subsided and he understood those were her sneakers rattling behind him.

"Where can we go? How do we get there?" Jackie asked, gripping the sleeve of Adrienne's henley as if she might know the answer. "How much money did you get back there at the restaurant? Adie, tell me you're coming. But you can't. You're too young. You have to go home. You'll get out, someday. You'll grow up and be free. Montreal! I know some dancers working there."

"Good," said Adrienne, and then again, "GOOD!" over the screech of an incoming train.

Upstairs at the station she pulled out her credit card and purchased Jackie's train ticket to Montreal. For a while they stood at a kiosk, obeying the instinct to share something ordinary—a Snickers bar—before saying good-bye. When he had thrown away the wrapper, she stood as swanlike as she could to hand him the journal, the money tight between the pages, and watched him carry the book through the hordes of people as if it were air, as if it cost her nothing to see it go. Finally she gave a flick of her head, the frizz flopping sideways, a discordance, a nearly perfect mistake.

OLD INN DOOR

THE BEST TIME FOR MY SISTER and me to visit our mangy pet rabbit's wilder cousins is dusk on the moistest days of crocus season. We leave Poindexter at home in his outdoor corral, meditating over the prickly grass. After looping around on our bikes awhile, we veer onto the grounds of the old hotel with the grandly dilapidated wraparound porch, from where a ramp descends in a U-shaped curve all the way to a sunken delivery station. We like to wheel lazily into this tunnel, Jewel and I, ticking out of waning daylight into pitch-blackness, our bikes as side by side as we can keep them down the slope, our elbows knocking together. It's all echo and chill and a shy, musty skitter. We spend a scary minute trying to find a hair clip we lost, groping bravely along until our eyes have made the shift and we can nearly see again. Generally there isn't too much to look at—just the grayish double doors and two ironing boards and finally a kicked-around metal finger splint with sticky foam

OLD INN DOOR

lining. The hotel's not a hotel anymore. It's all boarded up, although the lawn is well tended, better tended than ours, thick and green. Rabbits burrow on these grounds—hundreds of them, not wild ones, exactly, and not black and white like Poindexter, but feral broods of lop-ears, nesting under the porch amid torn-apart lattice and immense, untended lilac bushes. The old rabbit hutch still totters on stilts on the porch, its mesh doors loose on rusty hinges. "There's a coffeepot in here!" Jewel once exclaimed. It made us giddy with laughter, then shivery. And tonight there's a yellowish glow in the tunnel, a flat smear of light where the doors are ajar.

"Hang on," I say, so we straddle our bikes to listen a minute. Jewel trumps me, as always. Whenever I'm about to act in poor judgment, she talks me out of it. But if I'm not about to act that way, she dares me to.

"Go in," she urges.

"Not on a school night," I resist, even though it's practically June already, all our unenforced curfews completely forgotten.

"You know you want to," she boasts.

"So?" I ask.

"Oh, forget it."

"Why? Forget what?"

"You're right, Jaclyn. It'd be dumb to go in."

So we park our bikes and hoist ourselves onto the loading dock, brushing damp off our knees while peering over the threshold. All we see is a hallway leading up and away, like the school art teacher's lesson in perspective. If we walk up it, we'll get smaller. Far enough, we'll disappear.

"Girls!" I call. "Come back, little girls!"

Jewel clutches my arm. The hallway echoes, "Little girls!"

"Come out come out!" we call together.

At once an old lady appears in the hallway, not the enthusiastic bowlegged one who half jogs, half walks past our house every day, but a lanky one, dressed in men's plaid pajamas and flannel men's slippers, smoking a cigarette. All three of us scream: Jewel, the old lady, and me. The old lady is our grandma, who died last year in her sleep, wearing those same men's plaid pajamas, in her ramshackle house that smelled like roasted chicken, on the cornfield side of town, the side that throbs orange when the sun goes down. She was buried the morning after she died, our parents leaving home in the darkest-colored shirts they could find in their closets, and coming back an hour later with her mantel clock.

When we're all done screaming there in the tunnel, Grandma says, "Remember when I made you those finger puppets?" and then she waggles her fingers.

"What about them?" I ask.

I'm not being rude. This is the way we talked to our grandma, the way she liked us to. She was buried, we imagined, in her favorite denim overalls, her hair a silvery coil that's maybe still growing. They were peanut-headed finger puppets. She took a bulby half of a peanut shell, drew a little face on it, and stuck her finger up the neck hole. And then, ten more puppets, since Grandma had an extra pinky on one hand. We all grin at the memory—Grandma's peanut-headed fingers staging a food fight with frozen peas, yelling in hilarious peanut voices, pretending to be our parents arguing. "I'll fruggin kill you if you don't fruggin fruggin fruggin fruggin frugging frug," yelled one of the puppets.

"I'll fruggin creep on yur fruggin frug," improvised the peanut that was supposed to be our father, launching a pea.

"Frug yur creep'n fruggin frug!"

"Frug yur head. I'll fruggin blow yur creep right outta yur fruggin heinie with that fruggin hair dryer, you turn that fruggin thing on."

"Yeah, right. I'm goin' home! Girls, come on."

"We're already home," Jewel had densely pointed out at this juncture in the puppet show, since we weren't at Grandma's house the night she made the puppets. We were in our own kitchen. She was babysitting us. Frozen peas skidded under the oven and made bright-green spots on the floor days later, and stuck to the soles of our dad's big shoes.

"Oh, yeah, like yur gonna take the girls with you, are you? Like last time, right? Fruggin liar. Take the kids, hah! My hcinic! Fruggin liar."

"My heinie," Jewel had softly repeated, enjoying Grandma's spin on our mom and dad's vocabulary.

"I'm sorry I did that," Grandma says now on the loading dock threshold, the floor wax making ghosts on the floor behind her. "I should never have repeated those awful things."

"It was funny," I promise. "We laugh about it practically every night."

Jewel nods.

"Like heck it was," Grandma says.

Her cigarette smoke has no smell. Nor her pajamas, nor her silvery braid. But when she bends for a hug, her lanky frame is as gentle but firm as always, and when she steps back and closes the doors between us, it's with her usual tenderness. She's right about the puppets. We hardly speak of them at all, and even less about the poem we once swore we'd remember about Bess the landlord's daughter, after whom she was named.

"What's a highwayman?" I'd asked.

"What's a love knot?" asked Jewel.

"Hair ribbons, I guess."

We get on the wrong bikes, Jewel on mine and I on Jewel's, and ride them back up the ramp to find the crocuses stouter than candles, the rabbits safe in the shadows, the flat trees vivid against the sky. At home we spot the soccer-ball shape of our bunny alert in the circle of streetlight that floods his corral, whiskers quivering, waiting for rescue. It's my sister's turn to lift him, his belly wobbly in her arms, and carry him down to his pen in the cellar. I carry the apple. When Poindexter sneezes, he jumps right off the ground. Now he closes his teeth on the stem of the apple, lifts the whole globe of fruit off the bare cement, and drops it onto his bedding, where he thinks it belongs. For some time he nibbles and chews and we watch, not doing our homework, and not even eating our suppers that night. He believes Jewel and I are four rabbits: our feet their bodies, the whole rest of us their ears. We'll never leave him alone in the yard again. And never again will we pedal onto the hotel grounds. We'll keep to the opposite side of the road. At the faintest sign of anyone, we'll just keep riding, riding, riding.

FRANKIE D

KENNETH MARTIN MUELLER, who had just turned thirteen, and his grandmother, Gayle Pilsbury, were eating lunch on the screened porch of Gayle's new husband George's house when a tennis ball thumped down the short flight of concrete steps and rolled beneath the TV stand. It was July. The TV wasn't on in the middle of the day. Gayle forbade it. She also forbade Kenneth to call her new husband Grandpa, which was okay with Kenneth even though he had never met his real grandpa, who died before Kenneth was born. The resemblance was striking, people said—both Kenneth and his Grandpa James had sand-colored hair and a short, compact build. They were furtive, industrious, neat, and self-sufficient . . . but also given to private, inarticulate manias and peculiar fits of reverie. Grandpa James had had no favorite color, no favorite book, no favorite food, not even a favorite activity in particular, except being free of disarray and discomposure,

Gayle remembered, but his creased eyes and keen posture gave him a romantic, seafaring air no matter what he was doing. Ballroom dancing? She'd always felt the whole ocean liner swaying underneath them if they were waltzing to and fro.

Kenneth's favorite color was Halloween orange, which he imagined projected an air of moving purposefully along at a distance, like a sun on a horizon. He wore no other color. Secretly, Gayle thought he looked like a jailhouse inmate, she told Kenneth, who understood that what she meant by *secretly* was that she wouldn't gang up against him by taking his high-strung mom's side. She went on to say that once, when she was walking the dog in Oberlin, Ohio, where she and Grandpa James had lived, she came upon a group of prison inmates out for a stroll. Dressed in orange jumpsuits, they were gathered at the corner of Cedar and Morgan Streets, waiting to cross to the mulberry-spotted trail that would take them past the reservoir into the woods. One of the inmates, Hendy Jones, was a social acquaintance of Gayle's, for he had once been James's colleague, a professor at the college. He was in prison because he had too much to drink one night, stole a car belonging to one of his students, and then traded the car for sexual favors in an alleyway in Cleveland. The two of them, the rangy ex-professor and the diminutive Gayle, had tipped their hats to each other there on the frowsy, shaded corner of Cedar and Morgan Streets, which is to say they exchanged polite, even gallant, hellos.

The funny thing, Gayle admitted, was that this couldn't possibly have happened, not even in liberal, progressive-thinking Oberlin. No matter how gallant or well behaved, no inmates were allowed on strolls through town, chaperoned or not, and definitely never on outings past the verdant, wooded reservoir into the arboretum with its muddy creek, its tagged but untended botany experiments, its footpaths twisting between curtains of grass and willow.

The episode went hand in hand with Gayle's foot-in-mouth blunders about the finality of death, she confided in her grandson. Years after anybody had died, Gayle's first impulse on being face-to-face with a surviving relative was to ask how the dead person was doing these days, just as if they were still alive.

"How's Ellie?" she asked a friend whose sister had recently passed away.

"How *is* Tipper?" she had needed to stop herself from asking somebody whose freckled daughter's ashes had been scattered two decades ago.

"I wonder how James is doing," she often caught herself speculating, and then she'd hear his faint voice answering, *Not much going on in these parts, I'm afraid, my darling darling.*

It wasn't that she thought of James as being in some heaven or afterlife or still walking the face of the earth without her, she explained to Kenneth. She simply wanted to know how the dead people *felt* about being dead, like whether they were restless and discontented or were okay with it, especially in winter when it was cold, or in summer when the days were long. Most of them got used to it, she liked to think. They politely accepted no longer being around, and wore their shapeless, pointless clothing gladly enough.

The tennis ball was Frankie D's signal that he wanted to play. The dog knew better than to step onto the porch while meals were being served, but that didn't stop him from speaking his mind. He was nineteen years old. Kenneth's parents, who lived in Milwaukee, had bought the dog to keep Gayle company in Ohio after James died, and to nuzzle her into some semblance of having a normal day when all she wanted to do was lie there. Frankie D the puppy had lapped up her tears, Gayle recalled. And he had been at her side whenever she found herself dressing for James's departmental picnics, to which Gayle was still invited even after the point at which James would have long since retired and the two of them gone gallivanting off into old age.

At one of these faculty picnics, she met George, who smelled like the sea but who lived, of all places, just several hours north of where her daughter, Meredith, Kenneth's mother, lived with her family in Wisconsin. George was in Oberlin visiting friends. The long-distance courtship lasted just a month before he asked Gayle to marry him, and she insisted he drive to Ohio to get her so she wouldn't need to put Frankie D on a plane. Because of her hands, Gayle no longer drove, but she could still sightsee. Unluckily, not long after the drive to Wisconsin, George lost his license too, the result of spells of dizziness caused by years of trap shooting, the gun barrel ricocheting into his ear.

The house George had built for his retirement sat atop a grassy hill sloping down to a creek. Across the creek lay pasture for a small herd of buffalo belonging to a game farm, which was why George had chosen that lot for his house—because he intended to grow old gazing at something that was meant to outlast him. The animals stayed all together in a low, brown, woolly cloud. If the cloud wasn't in sight, you were supposed to be waiting for it to crest into view, and if it was in sight, you were expected to appreciate the sight of it—watch the breeze comb the dark curly locks, watch the grass get cropped beneath, watch the buffalo lift their massive heads and suddenly thunder away, spooked.

"You play with him and I'll clear up," Gayle said when she and Kenneth finished eating the crusts of their sandwiches.

Gingerly she stacked the dishes onto the tray while Kenneth scooted for the tennis ball and whistled for Frankie D. The trick was to throw the ball far enough down the slope to give the dog a run for his money, but not so far he struggled on his way back up. Kenneth rolled the ball sideways along a shaved ridge. Frankie D never actually ran anymore. He just sort of loped, showing off his new green collar. His real name, Franklin Delano, was etched onto the tag. He couldn't seem to see or smell the creek or the buffalo, and he couldn't hear the dishes clatter in the sink, and when he finally reached the ball, he never picked it up. Instead he spent a long time nosing it back to Kenneth's grandmother all the way in the kitchen, one fetch being enough for a Saturday afternoon.

SINCE KENNETH'S LAST VISIT in the spring, his grandmother's hands had grown noticeably more crooked and more, as she put it, patriotic—the knobs whiter than before, the palms pink, the fingertips bluer. The rest of her was still pixieish, dressed in the usual slender sweater, the trim capris, which in Grandpa James's day were called pedal pushers because you could ride bikes in them without getting your pant legs stuck in the gears, which came to mind whenever Kenneth was on his way to visit her, and the flat, doll-like shoes.

And she still wore all six of her rings—the original engagement ring from James, the second engagement ring from George, the original wedding band, the second wedding band, the square topaz from George, and finally her favorite, the delicately entwined lizard with the onyx eyes, from James. And although George had heated the porch and arranged for storm windows to be installed, she was never without a hand warmer, passing the teabag-looking object from one clawlike hand to the other even as she ate lunch or turned the pages of a book. George's house had included no bookshelves before Gayle moved in, but now, a year later, there were two respectable sets, along with some cubbies George had hammered into the back of a closet. Most of James's books had been donated to the Oberlin College library, but Gayle had plenty left over, mainly biographies. She kept the overflow in cardboard boxes on plastic sheeting in Kenneth's parents' basement.

Whenever Kenneth came visiting, he brought over a fresh biography to be exchanged with one from his grandmother's limited shelves. He and Gayle liked to start out Sunday mornings by looking at the captioned black-and-white photographs in the middles of them. You weren't supposed to choose which book to look at. You were supposed to let it choose you. This morning's selection, the biography of a ghost-story writer, contained snapshot-like photos of an embarrassed-looking person scrunched up in a wooden sled; a woman wearing a man's shirt while hunkered over a desk surrounded by "as many as a thousand books"; and some deranged-looking children playing musical instruments. There was the requisite wedding-feast photo and a close-up of the ghost-story writer wearing winged eyeglasses, one eye in "haunting" darkness and the other "peering out." Other books contained gentlemen sporting tall fur hats, pictures of snowy railroads and bridges being built, a picture of a lady suspended from the wing of an airplane, a small figure seated atop a camel, and two people playing Go.

But George had mixed feelings about thirteen-year-old boys sitting around looking at pictures of dead people in books. What Kenneth's mother and father didn't know wouldn't hurt their college-educated sensibilities, he said, and that was that: Kenneth was going out pheasant hunting for the afternoon, with George and his friend and the friend's dog. George was going to make a proper male chauvinist gun-toting Republican swine out of Kenneth, he teased, leading Kenneth to the closet with the book cubbies in it.

"Or at least make a Joe of you," he added, unknotting the top of a Hefty bag and pulling out a pair of black rubber boots that had been made for fighting the Korean War.

"Were they yours?" Kenneth asked.

"Of course. They *are* mine. They're my Mickey Mouse boots. Really. That's what they're called," George answered happily, holding up the heavy boots. The US Army would never make a warmer pair, he said. "You know India rubber balls?" George asked. Kenneth didn't. That was the kind of rubber the boots were made of. Someone standing in a supermarket checkout line had once offered George a hundred and fifty dollars for the boots, which were so enormous that Kenneth could fit his feet with their orange sneakers on inside them. The steely grommets were as big as fish eyes, and since Kenneth was so short, the boots tied up all the way to his knees. They looked impressive on him in the mirror, but funny when he peered at them from above, as if he were made of the top and bottom halves of two separate bodies, neither body his own. Plus, the boots weighed more than he did. No hawk would swoop down from a telephone wire and pluck Kenneth off the ground when he was wearing them, George said, and if Kenneth got lost in the corn rows, he could use them for shelter.

"But did you fight in them?" Kenneth wondered.

"Yes, he fought in them," Gayle called from the porch, where she was trying to pour some hand lotion into a special lotion-warming gadget that George had bought her. She dropped the bottle, needed both crippled hands to pick it back up, dropped it a second time, and finally let Kenneth pour the lotion into the gadget and flip the warming switch to ON. "But you don't want to get him going about the fighting," she warned.

"Yes, he does," said George.

"If I want to, I'll ask you," Kenneth compromised.

Frankie D was much too old to hunt and had never been a field dog, but George's friend's dog was a trained retriever. The friend came to get them in an old but immaculate Buick with stiff plastic seat covers. The old men folded themselves into the front seat while Kenneth slid in back amid piles of blaze-orange vests and hats, glad to be out-oranged for a change. He wore his long blond hair in a ponytail, and if he slipped the ponytail through the hole at the back of one of the orange caps, the cap stayed on. The vest tied at the sides and had a bright netted pocket. In the pocket, he discovered a hand warmer, still wrapped in its colorful package, the granules not yet activated.

George's friend drove so slowly that George joked he could run into somebody's farmhouse, fix a bag lunch, and be back in the car before it reached the next mailbox, and when they finally turned onto a dirt road leading into the hunting grounds, Kenneth reached out the window and captured an inchworm off its thread. One of the roads they passed on the way was where Kenneth's parents turned off to drive to their marriage retreats after dropping him at Gayle's. George pointed it out. There was a railroad crossing and an overpass. The retreats were for couples who had children, which meant that there were always at least six other children whose parents were on the same big exercise mat as Kenneth's parents, his mother often reminded him by way of apology as they were setting out to drop him at her mom's.

Kenneth planned on threading the inchworm onto a fresh tree when they got out of the Buick, but they parked on a road with cornfields to both sides, the stalks not yet mown, the fields glittering with straw-colored sunlight, so he kept it in his hand. The men put on their vests and hats and circled around to the car trunk, which they fumbled with a minute, not having the correct key. Finally they popped open the massive lid—and out of the trunk jumped a golden retriever like something shot live from a cannon. Kenneth was both relieved and disappointed to see only two guns in there. He wasn't going to shoot, it turned out. The old men pulled on leather gloves, then took them off again in order to load. The retriever bounded around in the ditch between the road and the cornfield, thrilled to be free. When Kenneth reached to pet it, it ate the inchworm off his hand. Then it darted in zigzags back and forth across the road until the old men started off without taking half a second to explain to Kenneth what was going on. He was supposed to just know, by instinct. One old man tromped off in one direction along the side of the road while the other tromped off in the opposite direction along the same side, leaving Kenneth standing next to the car in a brilliant patch of sun.

"Stay where you are!" George called importantly over his shoulder to Kenneth.

"He's short," the friend said.

"Now go!" the friend called just a few seconds later, when at what was by now a sizable distance away from each other, the two old men turned sharply off the road, marched across the ditch with their guns carried crosswise over their chests, and disappeared among the rows of corn, not even the tops of their orange caps showing to lead the way.

Kenneth took the ditch in one leap and stepped into the space between two papery stalks. Since the ground was dry, he bent to unlace the boots and made his way out of them. *Not much here but us ears, my darling darling,* he heard his grandmother say in Grandpa James's calm voice.

It was a different world in there. The only thing around was corn. The ground was hard dirt and the blue of the sky was soon gone from view, hidden by the papery crowns of the plants and all their fanned-out husks and tassels. Kenneth needed to do a breaststroke in order to keep his hat from getting knocked off his head. He couldn't have been happier. The only sound was dry leaves and the swish of his jeans. He couldn't hear a thing from the two old men, and the sure knowledge that they had either forgotten him or were trying to teach him to be a proper Wisconsin male was deeply amusing. Meanwhile the retriever kept crashing into his legs, nose to the ground, tail spinning like a propeller. The retriever's name was Louie, but he responded with the same delirious unconcern to whatever Kenneth called him. Hey, Index! Hey, Pistol! Hey, Third Eye! he called.

When the corn rows came to an end, and Kenneth stood on a ribbon of bristly grass, he found the old men conferring under a stand of trees. In the distance stood a silo and a barn the size of Kenneth's fingernail.

"You want to step back into that corn again and march in that direction," George's friend instructed Kenneth. "I'll take these trees and George'll follow the strip. And if you hear shots, quit walking until it's over. The dog goes nuts when he's birdy."

Over the next hour the sky turned pearly, the dry husks no longer flaming. Although the silo somehow failed to appear again after that first glimpse of it, Kenneth gradually acquired an understanding of what was expected of him. Namely, he was supposed to be doing exactly what he was doing, just walking through corn, not trying to be quiet. If a bird were to hear him and flush itself upward, one of the old men would shoot it. Ground swatting wasn't admirable. The bird needed to be trying to get away. It wasn't until they ended up back at the car, shared a Hershey bar, and trooped off into the adjacent field that Kenneth jumped at a loud, sudden squawking and a clapping of wings.

No shot went off. It turned out George's gun was jammed, though why his friend hadn't fired, George couldn't say. After waiting at the edge of the corn with Kenneth for several minutes, George reloaded and took an inquiring shot at the sky before calling his friend's name and Louie's.

No answering shot was fired, and neither man nor dog emerged.

"You stay here and I'll go in and look for him. Or I stay here and you go in," the exhausted George strategized, his mouth slackening.

So Kenneth marched back into the corn and made a couple of abrupt turns, peering down one corridor and then another, like someone searching for the drawing room. "Come, Jeeves!" he called. When he stepped back out, George too was missing, but Kenneth recognized the trees. Proud to be the lone orange speck on the serrated grass, he adored the idea that he knew where he was, that he had his own landmarks, his own code. The birds were like footballs balanced in the branches. He knew he cut a nice figure gliding along, the way he sauntered the hallways at school, everyone banging their lockers around him, their coats and backpacks flying, the buzzers buzzing, the hall clearing out just as Kenneth, unperturbed, got around to dialing his locker combination. A plane drew a broad arc across the sky, moving more slowly the farther away it got. He smelled cinnamon toast. Close by were some voices, and soon he came to the car, where the two old men were rummaging.

"Wanted a Coke," George explained, and he brought out a third Coke for Kenneth and zipped shut the cooler. His friend gave a sharp whistle. Louie scrambled up into the trunk and scooted into the spare-tire well as the lid came down.

Kenneth chose the trip home past the farmhouses for activating the hand warmer in his front vest pocket. Quickly the mixture of iron and carbon turned hot, and it was this chemistry that exerted the strongest hold on Kenneth as the rest of that day spun out . . . George's house empty on the ridge, Gayle's wailing and teeth-chattering down at the creek, her sodden sweater spread-eagled on the ground like a chalk outline of a murdered person, her rings showing their weight, two ambulances, two cops, his parents' tardy response because the rule of the marriage retreats was that phones were turned off during role-play. Kenneth's parents had been playing *themselves* at role-play, his mother explained to her friend by phone on the nighttime drive home to Milwaukee—themselves reenacting their first date, but then the second date had needed to be canceled, the two of them having to rush back to Gayle's.

And all along there was the pouch of fire blazing in the pocket of Kenneth's hunting vest, and Kenneth finally falling asleep underneath it as the road unspooled beneath him. His dream was of two buffalo. As in real life, Frankie D was drowned, his old dog body a clot of wet fur trapped against a sandbar in the creek where Gayle had tried and failed to reach him. The two buffalo in Kenneth's dream were Kenneth's parents on their first date. The buffalo who was his mother wore a dress of midnight blue, a set of bangle bracelets dangling from her tapered hoof where it rested against his father's lapel. His father's dreadlocked tail kept time to the music. The floor was church linoleum covered with exercise mats, in case anybody got tired of dancing.

AROUND THE CORNER and several blocks from Kenneth's parents' house in Milwaukee stood a small gabled house, with evergreen trees and gauzy curtains, crowded by other houses. A girl lived there, named Cicely. When he was seven and eight, Kenneth had had a crush on Cicely because she was smart and because of the way her humorous eyes turned instantly serious the second she was called on to answer a question in class.

Her house itself was feminine, cinched, and triangular, a dress with a bow. After school, if he took the long way home and the curtains were parted, which they usually weren't, he sometimes got a glimpse of her practicing piano. Her feet reached the pedals. She sat with her back to the window, and though her posture remained straight and the sound of the notes never reached the sidewalk, her hair swung with the intensity of her playing. Kenneth didn't dare pause as he walked along, but nonetheless his look was brazen enough that had she swiveled on the bench he would have caught her eye.

Before third grade, Cicely was switched to Sacred Heart School, and a short while later, Kenneth stopped walking on her street. Now and then he heard somebody mention her name or that of her parents, and once he thought he caught sight of her riding her bike, her hair fluttering in a way that bore no relationship to the breeze. Though he took it on faith he would run into her someday again, he didn't exactly care if this happened or not. So he was only mildly interested to learn, sometime over the weeks following Frankie D's drowning, that Cicely was to be a student in the youth strength-training class in which his mother had enrolled him at the YMCA. Kids under fourteen weren't allowed to use the weight and aerobics equipment until they passed the course.

Kenneth missed the first meeting because he was grounded. A kid had waved a knife at Kenneth on the way home from school, and Kenneth got in trouble for not telling his mother. The kid was decent enough, overweight, not too bright, and jealous of Kenneth the way a lot of boys were, simply for being himself. Just a day earlier, Kenneth had stopped wearing orange. With as little fanfare as when he had started, he had gotten out of bed and put on a pair of silvery basketball pants and a steel-colored turtleneck. No one commented to him about it up front, but there was a buzz in the air in the midst of which Kenneth's friends, who called him Ken, not Kenneth, became the objects of a renewed, vicarious popularity. The small band of them—Kenneth, Sally, Ingrid, and Mohammed—were walking home from school along Hazel Avenue, just passing the construction site for a new retirement community, when the kid, Brian Hoorst, appeared from around some pallets of building materials, pulled out the knife, and waved the blade inches from Kenneth's throat.

The other kids just stood there, mortified for Brian, who in addition to being fat endured the reputation of having a dad who wore bowling shoes to parent-teacher conferences.

"I don't swing that way, Brian. Nothing personal," Kenneth had said. Then they all started walking away, Ingrid, in her inside-out Moosehead Beer sweatshirt, bringing up the rear. Brian ducked through a gap in the security fence and became camouflaged by grayness, dimness, and undoneness. It was one of the girls' mothers who called Kenneth's mother to tell her what had happened, and then Kenneth's mother who called the police. On further reflection some days later, she turned on Kenneth, as angry at him for not telling her that he had been "assaulted" as she was worried Brian might come back and really slash him the next time.

"He's more likely to come back now that the police are after him than if you'd left him alone," said Kenneth, regretting saying this at once. He knew his mother's winces, their stages of profundity. According to his father, Meredith was always seeking out the rationale behind her feelings, and rating them according to some hierarchy that reconfigured itself whenever anyone else got close to being able to figure it out. Recently, she'd completed six weeks of radiation therapy for breast cancer. The hospital was spired, arched, and gargoyled. Walking into it each day, she would then be led by nurses to the locker room, where other patients commingled beneath a vast ceiling. Then the busy young technicians would call her name, position her body inside a white room, stop what they were doing, look into her eyes, compliment her on her stamina, and tell her things about their boyfriends. When her course of treatment was done, it was like she'd been exiled from the kingdom. Now she told Kenneth, "You have the *power*," imagining Brian jumping on Kenneth in retaliation for her phoning the cops, and then Kenneth's pardon of the boy. Tonight was early dinner, and soon she would be on her way to her teaching job, with her blotted mascara, her self-blacking eyes.

"I can handle him. Don't worry about it," Kenneth told her. "Brian's cool with it. We talked."

"You talked?" Meredith believed every word he said.

Immediately she phoned the district attorney.

"I'm Kenneth Martin Mueller's mom. Meredith Martin Mueller. I have here a 'Notice to—'" she knocked around on the desk a minute in search of the afternoon's mail. "A 'Notice to Victim of Case Processing, Intake Case Number 7958,' which says that, hmm, the case is being forwarded to the district attorney's office for their review. But I'd like to say that Brian, the kid, the boy who pulled the knife . . . yes, but also a disorderly conduct charge. But he's no longer behaving in a disorderly fashion. Brian Hoorst . . . in fact, yes. So we feel that to continue with these charges would be a mistake all around, because then he might—exactly. So if the, the DA would get back in touch—yes—okay, thank you very much."

"But Brian's still really screwy," Kenneth amended, the second the phone call was over.

His mother turned stock-still, her hand in the air. All possible misunderstandings and their potential consequences scrolled past her expression like oranges and bananas in a slot machine. It was hilarious. She sent Kenneth to his room, banning him from strength-training class for that first week, the ironical consequences of *that* decision already whipping past her eyes.

So he had been first to show up in the gym at the Y for the following week's class, his mother being in such a guilty hurry to get him there. It was while he was looking at the wall of mirrors, watching somebody reflected in them performing a set of grueling midair push-ups while suspended from what looked like a giant rubber band, that the door next to the Gatorade vending machine swung open, and in walked Cicely.

Show up, pay attention, speak the truth, and don't be attached to results, a caption for a photograph in one of Gayle's biographies came back to him. Cicely's hair was as all over the place as it had been in second grade, but it was sort of roped in as required.

Kenneth drew himself up. At thirteen, Cicely was a dismaying sight. Her neck was too bony, her face too thin, her nose too pointed, and her ears too big. And the rest of her was . . . *flat. Just flat. The narrows* . . . Kenneth heard the voice of his Grandpa James shouting, *Throw her a rope!* even though James had never actually been a seafarer, had only smelled like one—bracing, stinging, deep.

Not appearing to notice Kenneth, Cicely took her place near the water fountain, which was where the kids had been instructed to line up. Or maybe she allowed just a flicker of the eyes, as if to say, "So there." When a safe number of other classmates had lined up beside her, Kenneth got in line too. He was proud of his hint of mustache, but he stopped his eyes from straying to it in the mirror. Considering the kind of man he intended to be, it would be wrong to condemn Cicely for his new mustache being beside the point. *Too long for what?* he scolded himself, when he and the class took turns with the weights and pulleys. Her neck was too long for *what?* Her arms too gangly for what? Her nose too sharp for what?

At break he bought two Gatorades from out of the machine and presented one to Cicely.

"So what are people praying for at Sacred Heart these days?" he asked her.

Cicely had rabbit teeth.

"Oh, you know," she said. It must be hell to be a girl at thirteen still looking like you're eight, Kenneth imagined himself consoling her.

"Why does it quench your thirst?" he asked. "How is Gatorade different from water?"

Her expression turned serious just as he had remembered, then menacing.

"Ions," she answered in a vampire voice. "HELP! It's radioactive!" she screeched, flopping backward on one of the mats so her tank top hiked up to reveal an outie belly button, and grabbing an exercise ball for abdominals, the next part of class. She was always the leader. He found his own ball, dragged one of the mats to the glass overlooking the swimming pool, and lay back to deliver his gaze into the high, fluorescent space.

IT WOULD BE the following May, at George's eightieth-birthday celebration, before Kenneth saw his grandmother again.

Big-band music was playing on the stereo, the speakers arrayed on the flat ridge of lawn amid tables of catered food underneath a striped awning on tilted poles. Some rows of stout new evergreens had been planted at the bottom of the slope, not exactly obscuring the view of the creek but fringing the banks, and breaking the sandbar into tidier-looking splashes than before. For months, while George and Gayle wintered in Phoenix, the herd of buffalo had also been away, shipped off to whatever climate bison-burgers-to-be got shipped to in winter, and George had begun to resign himself to the animals not returning home in time for his party.

But early that morning the barest glimpse of the herd, just a ripple of brown, could be seen from over the distant hill, and now the whole woolly cloud of them floated near, where the guests could admire them and drink to George's vigorous enjoyment of their territory. Gayle looked frailer than before, especially by comparison with George. The rushing creek had done her harm. Even so she was still pixieish, her rib cage brave under a V-neck tunic, the six rings bulging against her knuckles. She and George would never have made the trip to Phoenix for the winter had Frankie D been alive, she never tired of reminding everybody, never wistfully but with a fresh, wondrous jolt of unhappy surprise.

Kenneth wasn't the youngest at the party by far, for there were all sorts of cousins from George's family in Texas.

Generally speaking, other kids didn't come near Kenneth unless he made some welcoming gesture, after which they wouldn't leave him alone if their lives depended on it. Sometime soon he would get out the new four-wheel and organize rides, but for now he was on his usual guard, mainly keeping an appropriate distance away from his parents—his mother pregnant in a clingy dress, his father loading her plate with all the fattening things they didn't dare keep at home. Fried chicken and gobs of potato salad crowded the plates. Cake too, because George believed in cutting into it right away instead of waiting for people to be too stuffed to enjoy it.

On the cake was an icing photo of George, in which he was noticeably older than James in the photos Gayle had saved of her first husband, swashbuckling images that Kenneth would someday turn out to look like. It made him proud to harbor this inside view of things and to know that Gayle disliked photos on birthday cakes because they were in color. Color photographs cheapened things, she had explained to Kenneth earlier that day, before the caterers arrived. Her least favorite books were the ones that people who didn't know her very well tended to give her as gifts, knowing she read biographies. If the photos were in color, their human subjects didn't *count,* she said; that is, they'd never join that sepia throng drifting peaceably around, hybrids of ghosts and memories.

Some bottles of brandy had wound up on the wheeled cart on the screened porch, and since Meredith had been still in bed, sleeping, Gayle asked Kenneth to pour her some. Kenneth's dad was on the lawn helping George set up for the party. What did Kenneth remember of the day Frankie D drowned, Gayle had suddenly wondered.

"Your sweater lying on the ground and my mom saying hand warmers are poison," he had answered without hesitation.

"They are if you eat them," Gayle said through a welling of tears, and told him how she had thrown the ball sideways on the ridge, just like Kenneth did, only it hadn't gone sideways, instead it had rolled down the hill, right into the creek.

It was awful to watch her cry, yet impossible for Kenneth to stroke or embrace her. Goodnight kisses had been all that had ever passed between them, and besides, she was too crushable looking. She kept telling him she was sorry, lifting her glass in a puzzled way. Sorry, she meant, not for weeping but for letting Frankie D go. She meant "letting him go" as in down to the creek and also as in dying, and she meant "sorry" as in regret and also as in sorrow.

"But I got what I deserve for my carelessness," she claimed, "having to go on living without him."

"But you have George," Kenneth ventured, like a grown man might.

"I'm glad to have met George," Gayle agreed, turning the lizard ring on her finger, the onyx eyes brightly spotting. "But Frankie D was the love of my life, you know," and then she said it again in a less drunken way that he would hear later on in James's voice at the party: *Frankie D. Frankie D was the love of her life.*

Aware now of his hands in his pockets, his ponytail meeting the fold of his shirt collar, Kenneth waited for his grandmother to make her way through the party to where he was standing. Because of her hands being bent out of shape, the less she drank, the more she spilled. By the time she reached

Kenneth, which turned out to be much, much later, after the young cousins had pleaded for his company on the four-wheel rides, her glass had been refilled but she was sober again.

"So, Kenneth," she asked, "are you interested yet in girls?"

He told her he was.

"And do you have a girlfriend?"

"I'm not sure," Kenneth answered.

She gave him a look, reading the way he put a finger to his hint of mustache, which felt like a shadow, a tactile blur. From over the ridge came a fragrance of buffalo dung. The music was turned higher, and Kenneth's parents were the first ones dancing.

"I mean, I do sort of have one, only it's taking her a long time to figure it out," Kenneth explained.

The image came to him then, as it did frequently, of Cicely's outie belly button, along with the notion that he disagreed with Gayle that people were okay with being dead. They might pretend to be okay but they'd be going insane. He imagined himself in one of those books and poor clueless Cicely turning the pages, her socks slipping into the heels of her shoes. His grandmother nodded when Kenneth blushed. Eventually she glided off, and then after a minute, George walked by.

"Been meaning to ask you about my war boots," he called to Kenneth. "Have any idea where I might find them?"

Gayle didn't head for the rest of the party. Instead she swerved toward the door leading into the porch, which opened from within as if somebody had been waiting there for her. There was a glint of indiscernible color as the door swung shut, the somebody staying on the other side.

CHOIR PRACTICE

Ellen didn't plan on punching Betsy in the nose, at least not until the idea suddenly came to her. The girls were expected to play Marco Polo, an activity that Betsy's parents and Ellen's recently widowed dad thought was a good way for eight-year-old girls to get to know each other.

"What is there to know about us?" Betsy asked in a deadpan voice as the girls approached the kidney-shaped swimming pool. "What we see is what we get."

She shrugged, eyeing not Ellen but the flapping door of the pool skimmer, as if it might suck her in, like the toads it was her job to scoop out of the basket. Promptly the girls sat on the very first step, up to their belly buttons in water, and began inching down toward the second step. It was a chilly, gray day, which made sense to them both since this day in the Rassmusens' swimming pool, this lemonade party, as their parents called it, had been promised all week, a week of glorious sunshine that had come to a halt that morning, just as both girls expected it to.

Ellen was impressed. Never had she felt such kinship as she did with Betsy Rassmusen. The two little girls were perfectly alike. They were squat, plain, reliable B and C pupils whose clothing was always out of style but in a respectable, eye-catching way. That morning, Ellen had put on a faded sundress of red Scotch plaid, which turned out to match, exactly, in fabric as well as in style and cut, right down to the indifferent-looking sash and the crooked row of rickrack, the dress worn by Betsy's doll.

Betsy had been carrying the doll around when the doorbell rang, and it was the second thing Ellen noticed after Mr. and Mrs. Rassmusen ushered her and her dad inside their house. The first thing she noticed was that Betsy was already wearing her swimsuit and cap. The cap had a yellow anemone on it. Earlier that morning, Ellen too had considered putting on her own new bathing cap but had managed to steer herself away from doing something so stupid. She was awed by Betsy's anemone, and at the same time she felt superior to it.

Betsy felt the same way. She loved her doll's dress, but she would never have dared to wear one like it herself. To see the plaid dress on this new girl, Ellen, filled Betsy with a mixture of admiration and disdain, a confusing emotion made even more confusing by both girls experiencing it at the same time.

"You're wearing my doll's dress," Betsy finally remarked.

"My mother made it for me," Ellen said.

"And then she died," Betsy said.

"It's in the past," Ellen said.

CHOIR PRACTICE

Look at the bright side and buck up and get on with your life in as normal a way as possible, Ellen's mother used to say, like when Ellen popped a robin's egg into her mouth and bit down on the crisp blue shell. They were walking around the swan pond in Heckshire Park, not far from where the Easter egg hunt had been held a week earlier, and Ellen mistook the robin's egg for a leftover Cadbury cream-filled one. At least it isn't a duck egg, her mother said.

The two girls gazed at each other in wary silence, engaged in the requisite staring contest, waiting to see what they should do and say next. They were equal to each other in this as well. If they hadn't been offered an ice cream sandwich, they might have stood in the front hall an hour longer. It was bad enough to be set up as new friends by their parents, but it was worse to slide too easily into that friendship.

"Does anybody want an ice cream sandwich?" Betsy's mom called.

Neither girl blinked.

"I'll have one," said Ellen's father. Three months after his wife's death, he was practicing being sociable for his daughter's sake. On the phone with other parents he still sometimes accidentally introduced himself as Ellen Flood's mom.

"Oh, okay, I'll have one," both girls called, and then they ate three ice creams each, hiding the wrappers in the bottom of the trash can in Betsy's bathroom so their parents wouldn't know.

"So do you play clarinet too?" Ellen asked.

"If your dad told you I do, then you already know I do, so why are you asking?" Betsy answered.

She led Ellen to her room, where a music stand faced the corner as if it were being punished for poor behavior. In the open case on the floor beside it lay an assortment of cracked clarinet reeds, from Betsy sucking too hard on the last of the bamboo flavor while doing her homework, just like Ellen sucked on *her* reeds, and two stiffened, forest-green, cable-knit kneesocks knotted together for swabbing the spit from inside the instrument, just like Ellen did with her socks.

Ellen looked around. All her trademarks were infringed on by this separate, other left-handed girl, this plagiarized Ellen, who felt just like Ellen did. *Copycat*, they both thought, but they knew better than to say it, fearing that the other might say it at the same time.

Had Betsy ever sat on her own birthday cake, Ellen wondered? Did she ever accidentally kick the gym teacher in the testicles? Was she left behind at the fire station when everyone else went home from the field trip? Did she once say "screw me" when she meant to say "excuse me"? Did she like to say "Jell-O" when she answered the phone? If she could have a dog would she name it Tuna? Did she ever get an A on somebody else's math test by mistake?

"I have to go to camp this summer," Ellen said.

"Lucky you," said Betsy in her monotone.

"I think we should go outside to the pool now and play Marco Polo," Ellen finally insisted, imagining that maybe in the swimming pool her and Betsy's similarities would achieve a purer form. They could be mer-girls. They could synchronize swim. They would stand on their hands for seven and a half seconds each, and then they would swim back and forth underwater, as side by side as fins on the same fish.

"Of course we should. That's why you're here," Betsy said.

Then she found the doll's swimsuit and undid the buttons down the front of the dress, revealing that the doll wore nothing underneath, not even underpants. Ellen was embarrassed, but whether for the doll's sake or her own, she didn't know. Under her own dress was her swimsuit, which she had put on that morning, not liking to strip past her underpants in front of other girls.

She hung her dress in the closet and, barefooted, allowed herself to be regarded. Betsy's gaze was as fierce and unforgiving as her own. They were both stubby girls with short arms, thick ankles, square feet, and goose bumps from shivering. In their two-piece swimsuits, they looked like dressed-up dachshunds. Because they were fond of their own bodies, they were able to appreciate each other's as well, especially in the water, which was warmer than the air, and which made them appear even squarer in shape. It was while they were inching farther down the pool steps, becoming squatter and shorter-waisted the farther in they got, that Ellen found herself about to strike her new friend. She imagined it would be like slapping herself—her hand meeting its punishing reflection, the water breaking all around but quickly smoothing itself across again, as clear and serene as it was before. She imagined it would make them feel alive inside their skins, her and this other girl, her and herself.

"Do you have a swimming pool too?" Betsy asked, putting on her swim goggles and handing Ellen an identical pair.

"No, but I'm a small part African American," Ellen boasted.

Betsy squinted. "Let's see it."

Ellen explained it wasn't visible to the naked eye, and that since it came from her mother's side of the family, it couldn't be seen in her father, either.

"Maybe in your hair," Betsy allowed.

No, never had either girl been understood so well by another human being. They had been understood by dogs, since dogs were great at understanding, but by other girls, never. Maybe by boys, but that still wasn't as good as by dogs. Sometimes it was discouraging to be understood by dogs better than you were understood by anyone else, but it was even more depressing not to be allowed to have a dog.

Not yet buoyant, and finding the water still warmer than the air, or maybe it was only the air getting cooler, the girls lowered themselves to the last step down. The skimmer door thumped with a drowned-sounding gurgle. When Ellen's hand arced backward Betsy recoiled, understanding instinctively what was to come. A shocked expression appeared behind the sheen of her swim goggles. The girls' parents had disappeared for a minute behind the pool shed, probably to smoke pot, since a tendril of purple smoke was wisping above it into the clouds. To one side of the pool stretched a chain-link fence, but the rest of the fence was made of woven slats of wood with trees spilling over. Inchworms lowered themselves on invisible threads, then yanked themselves impossibly upward again.

Just as the parents stepped back onto the patio, carrying stacks of psychedelic beach towels, Ellen swung.

Striking Betsy, it turned out, wasn't like slapping herself at all. Instead, Ellen and Betsy became two separate beings, no longer alike. Betsy slid underwater, the yellow anemone throbbing on the crown of her swim cap. Betsy's mom screeched. It was possible Betsy was only pretending to drown, but even Ellen found it difficult to tell. Ellen's dad, who to Ellen appeared to be mouthing the words "What's done is done so buck up and get on with your life in as normal a way as you possibly can," just stood there. Betsy's dad jumped feetfirst into the water, forgetting how shallow the shallow end was and breaking his finger on the edge of the pool. Betsy's mom called 911. Betsy's dad made a lunge for the yellow anemone but Betsy pulled hard away, her face ablaze with pain and fury, her nose spewing blood, the swim goggles half off, the blood clouding the water like after a frenzy of sharks.

Ellen was horrified. What had she done at her first lemonade party? Attacked her new double, her new, only friend, with whom she might have been like cousins for the rest of their lives.

She remained in the pool all during the rescue. Towels were unfolded, ice was held to Betsy's face, the three parents hovered over her. The ambulance was turned away. The lemons were squeezed into a slender glass pitcher gritty with sugar, and Betsy's dad winced from the bruise on his finger when he took up his glass. The cops, who'd shown up with the medics, hung around a while longer to sniff around and peer under the obvious surfaces of things, in search of other things that they might need to write about on their clipboards.

"Come here," they called. "Did you hit your new friend?" But Ellen only nodded dumbly, bobbing and treading, her swim goggles leaking. A light rain started falling, the umbrella was cranked up, and the last of the lemonade was poured into the glasses. Ellen made herself sink, stayed underwater for what felt like a week, and when she came back up, not even the doll was looking at her.

NOT QUITE TWENTY YEARS LATER, on the Sunday after her roommate's wedding, Ellen stood outside her town house waiting to be picked up by a bus carrying Diane Jackson's Community Choir for Teachers to their weekly choir practice. Since Ellen taught special ed she was eligible to join, and though she hadn't exactly signed on the dotted line yet, she was happy enough just to see what the choir was like.

Since it was sometimes cold at choir practice, Diane had suggested she dress in layers, so Ellen wore blue jeans, a blouse, a sweater, and a denim jacket under a rain poncho. She carried an umbrella against the driving rain, and in a plastic bag a pair of clogs, some replacement socks, and a copy of *The Haunting of Hill House* in case she decided to sit out the singing and read about poltergeists. Despite the dismal weather, which would have ruined Ellen's roommate's wedding if Ellen hadn't succeeded in persuading her to hold the wedding indoors even though it was June, Ellen had a good-weather song in her head. It was one of the sixth-grade choir songs from when Ellen was a girl. The verse she remembered went like this:

> *I'll be a dandy and I'll be a rover,*
> *You'll know who I am by the song that I sing,*
> *I'll something something something, I'll sleep in your clover,*

CHOIR PRACTICE

Who cares what tomorrow shall bring?
Oooh Oooh, Aaah Aaah, Oooh Aaah.

"I care what tomorrow shall bring," said Ellen to the rain.

As a child in the choir, she used to picture the *tomorrow* of the song as being like a chariot bringing things to other children, things like good grades, long legs, and big floppy-eared dogs. She didn't know what she wanted her new adult chariot to bring her, but now that her roommate was on her honeymoon, it had better be good.

At five to eleven, exactly on schedule, a bus rounded the corner onto Ellen's street, grinding to a halt in front of a woman wheeling a small piece of luggage along one of the many cockeyed driveways. The seemingly random arrangement of identical town houses was supposed to make the neighborhood interesting to look at, but instead it only caused Ellen regret, reminding her that the tract of land had once been a potato field redolent with manure, box turtles, red-winged blackbirds, and potato bugs that stank when you caught them and trapped them in jars. The woman who was just now climbing onto the bus resembled Ellen's feather duster, being straight and rather bony with an extravagant head of feathery pink hair.

When Ellen climbed aboard, the blast of heat nearly forced her out again. It was just like a sauna, complete with a fragrance of Bengay and vapor rub. Colgate toothpaste, she had learned from an email the teachers were sending around, was a good salve for burns, and there seemed to be some of that wafting around the bus as well.

She removed her backpack, rain poncho, denim jacket, and hand-knitted sweater and took a seat next to a young man who happened to be knitting something himself—a bristly yellow scarf, strongly resembling a Dr. Seuss character. Several of the teachers wore scarves like that, but Ellen found them Grinchy and Mayzie-birdish.

The young man, whose name was Bobbie, had a lovely symmetrical face with extraordinarily tired-looking eyes. His hair was blond dreadlocks but his beard was closely trimmed. The scarf was for his grandmother, he explained as the bus made a detour through Centerport and rumbled past the hillside comprising the Northport cemetery.

"Nice gift," said Ellen.

"It looks like a caterpillar," Bobbie conceded, "but it's the only thing I know how to make except for scrambled eggs."

By now Ellen was beginning to wonder if she was on the wrong bus.

First, Diane Jackson wasn't on it.

And it wasn't a school bus, as you might expect of a teacher's choir.

Many of the passengers spoke only with difficulty. Some wheezed, some coughed, some cleared phlegm. Bobbie's voice was velvety deep like those of the more mature boys in her long-ago sixth-grade choir, but if this were a choir, Bobbie would be the only one singing. While Ellen's sixth-grade choir had been an efficient, eager lot, today's motley gathering would never be able to "stop singing on a dime" the way Ellen's choir director used to require. Instead, today's gathering was more like what a choir might sing *about*, mournful yet strangely celebratory. Quite a few of the passengers were missing patches of hair.

The bus had wound its way to the expressway and started barreling west at seventy miles an hour through sheets of rain striking the windows.

"Yikes," said Bobbie, clapping the bristly scarf to his face. Then he started to laugh, and soon a lot of them were laughing, their ghoulish cackles and raspy hilarity reminding Ellen of the Halloween CDs in the shop where she moonlighted.

Just who were these people?

And where were they all going?

Ellen decided she wouldn't ask. And because she was still fighting against being the kind of person who said to herself things like, "Oh, get a grip, this is only the beginning and it's only getting worse and there's nothing you can do about it so you might as well buck up and make the most of it," she thought again of the song: Today, while the blossom still clings to the vine *(stop on a dime)*, I'll taste your strawberries, I'll drink your sweet wine *(stop on a dime)*. Oooh. Aaah."

"What are you singing?" Bobbie asked.

"I was only thinking about singing it," said Ellen, perplexed that he was able to read her mind, and then warming to him she told him about the time she had gone to the wrong birthday party and given the gift of a sewing basket to some kid she didn't know.

LATER THAT DAY when they had reached where they were going, Ellen would learn that the woman who looked like the pink feather duster, whose name was Marilee Washington, had diffuse cutaneous scleroderma.

    This meant that Marilee was gradually turning into a statue. Her skin was hardening and her joints, digestive system, heart, kidneys, lungs, and blood vessels would soon follow their example. She was almost always cold. Already her face was as tight as plastic (Marilee allowed both Ellen and Bobbie to touch it, and she demonstrated, by not being able to smile, the limits of its elasticity), while her esophagus had hardened so considerably that she had trouble swallowing. Poor wound healing as well as bleeding tendencies were in Marilee's future, as was a likelihood of congestive heart failure, lung destruction, and high blood pressure. With treatment she might last five years or so. In the meantime there were skin lotions, lubricants, and bath oils to help her through the days, along with blankets, special socks, heating pads, aspirin, ibuprofen, antacids, antibiotics, and maybe, someday, cortisone.

    "Don't worry, it's not contagious," she said, delivering one of her frequent nonsmiles while holding her cold arms stiffly in front of her for Ellen to help her put on her sweater. What with tie-ups near the Verrazano Bridge and an emergency beverage detour off Garden State Parkway, the bus trip had filled five rainy hours all the way to the boardwalk in Atlantic City, where it finally unloaded its weary but excited passengers under the dripping turquoise awning of the Tropics Hotel and Casino. After everyone checked into their rooms (luckily, there was an extra hide-a-bed available for Ellen in one of the suites) the group was herded into a banquet room for an orientation cocktail and the distribution of bonus casino tokens.

A large group then made for the slot machines while the other smaller groups chose among countless restaurants for supper. Bobbie opted for Hooters, but the wait would be an hour. Marilee said no to the KGB, owing to how cold it might be as a result of the bar being carved from solid ice, and no to the pricey Montreal Lounge.

Finally they settled on one of the more modest bar and grills, where they were given a table for three near a floor-to-ceiling window overlooking lines of gamblers cashing in their chips. A muffled sound of bells and buzzers ricocheted against the glass. Ellen had a Caesar salad, Bobbie ate two hamburgers, and Marilee barely sipped at a bowl of white chili. Her pink hair appeared to warm her, making her look like a troll doll on fire.

"And what do *you* have?" Marilee asked Bobbie. Bobbie answered that he had aplastic anemia but that he didn't feel like talking about it.

"What about you?" Marilee asked Ellen. "What do *you* have?"

Does aplastic anemia mean you're going to die? Ellen kept herself from asking. "They haven't diagnosed me yet," she said. With trepidation she scanned her salad plate, hoping there wasn't anything on it that a person with a mysterious, undiagnosed illness wasn't supposed to eat.

"When did your mom die?" Bobbie asked.

"When I was eight," Ellen answered before realizing he must have read her mind again. She hadn't said a word about her mom, not even when they were passing the Northport Cemetery, which was where she wished her mom was buried since it was prettier than the one in Huntington.

THE BELL AT THE END OF A ROPE

Then Bobbie's gums started bleeding and Marilee nearly choked on a kidney bean. "There's nothing crazier than real life, is there?" she said, catching sight of *The Haunting of Hill House* when Ellen opened her backpack to grab some wet wipes, and soon they were riding the elevator upstairs to recoup, the way sick people often needed to do. Ellen's suite was on a different floor, and when she got there somebody was wheezing in one of the beds and someone was sobbing in the bathroom.

"What do *you* have?" Ellen nearly asked.

"Are you okay?" she called, tapping gently on the bathroom door.

It turned out to be the maid, who hurried past Ellen and vanished down the hallway. Ellen sank into a chair near a small, round table on which lay a folder of hotel stationery. She pulled out the pen and a sheet of paper, holding it up in the direction of the lamp, in search of the watermark. There wasn't one, but the ballpoint pen was quill shaped. Outside the window, rain sluiced through the gutters. A vast puddle darkly trembled on the flat gravel roof as if in compensation for the view of the ocean being on the opposite side of the building.

"Dear Betsy," she wrote.

You were wrong. Camp is fun. It's good to be with other people for a change. I mean, maybe the other campers look at me and feel glad not to be me, but whenever I look at the girl with the tube coming out of her belly button or the girl with the bump on her neck or the kid who smells like rotten oranges or

CHOIR PRACTICE

the guy with the scales, I would rather have my problem than anyone else's. The food's okay but my tent mate can't eat chocolate. I'm sorry I punched you in the nose that day and I hope we can still get to know each other.

Your fateful friend,
Ellen Emma Flood

Ellen had meant to write *faithful*, not *fateful*. She didn't change it, though. As she often told her special ed students, mistakes sometimes turned out to be better in the end than the things they stood in for.

She folded the letter in three, sealed it in one of the flimsy white envelopes, and zipped the envelope in her backpack to bring home and mail to Betsy, who she hadn't seen or heard of since the day that Betsy's parents had gotten in trouble with the cops for smoking pot at the lemonade party. She took out her contact lenses, put on her glasses, and rode the elevator down to join Bobbie in the casino, where together they watched one of the horse races airing on the monitors that were placed amid the gaming tables. Colored lights spun across the huge, dark space, like a shower of bells in a whirling sky. Melting ice cubes glistened on the matted shag carpet. Ellen lost a hundred dollars in the slot machines, but when the band started playing, she and Bobbie slow-danced. After midnight she combed his hair, since it turned out the dreadlocks were from his being too tired to comb it himself, and she braided it into a ponytail. Then they tasted and drank each other a little like in the song about the strawberries and finally lay side by side on the hide-a-bed, her head on his shoulder, her fingertips toying with a leftover dreadlock.

The other suite mates came in and took turns in the bathroom. Ellen realized she would miss the next day at work. She'd have to call in a sub when morning came.

"I'm sorry you're sick," she said to Bobbie.

"I'm sorry you're sick too," he said.

MCGUFFEY'S THIRD ECLECTIC READER

THE DAY QUEEN ELIZABETH THE FIRST was eaten by the goat was the same day the earthquake laid waste to the public library. Countless books were mangled, crushed, warped, torn, twisted, soiled, stained, soaked, stolen, trod upon, or otherwise ruined, and although, to the girl's surprise, their loss meant little to her compared to the loss of the stout yellow library building, with its whitewashed shutters and shimmering steps, the quake might save her a little money were she to tell a lie. That is, were she to claim that she'd returned the queen to the library just before the earthquake struck, rather than having left her in the bicycle basket at the edge of the cove, where she was eaten by the goat, the girl, whose name was Wanda, and who lived in a place called Sandy Bay in the Windward Islands in the Caribbean Sea, might not be held responsible for paying a fine for the queen's destruction. With this in mind, it seemed possible, even likely, that Wanda had wittingly induced the goat's eating of Her Majesty, which was completely untrue, even though she missed the library building much more than she missed the books. There it stood in Wanda's heart: the bright yellow gone building. Its musty high dark passageways frosted with sun. The quaint requirement that you needed to put on shoes "prior to entering." The jumble of used pedicure flip-flops (the librarian's sister worked for a pedicurist at a neighboring cove) in a crate near the doorway in case you owned no shoes. The slap of flip-flops on wood, the rubber tabs poking upright between splayed toes, the oily brow of the unhappily plain librarian with her oily-looking ears. The pages of books pressing firmly against each other, the covers of books wedged tightly against each other, the spines of the books with their helpful rows of Dewey decimals lined up so near one another, the wooden cart with squeaky wheels, the smaller cart with quiet wheels but one of them crooked, the millions of words face-to-face with each other, only not any longer, and so on and so on, the yellow edifice still upright in Wanda's heart, but on earth no longer.

Whenever Wanda, engaged in research for the writing of her school report, had opened the book *Lives of the Monarchs: Hail to Good Queen Bess,* and come to the picture of the skinny-faced Bess with her starched doily collar, her hair as poofy as the cushions fixed to the chairs in the reading room (there were only two chairs, since the third was in use as a step stool, its cushion smuggled home by the librarian to make a pillow for her son), Wanda could hardly keep from growling, since what right had such a turkey-necked person as the chalky-faced queen to be written about in library books, when so many other, more handsome (darker) people were left completely out of them. Such a stickish-looking lady, in such silly, fancy clothes, written over and over again about. The queen's father, the king, had declared women unfit to be monarchs at all, which ended up being in Good Bess's favor, unfortunately, but which sufficed as the central argument of Wanda's report. The stolen cushion might have made it permissible to tell a lie about the book's return to the library, since lying to a librarian who stole cushions off chairs was better than lying to one who didn't, unless maybe it was worse, in God's eyes, to take advantage of that first falsehood by telling your own. Anyway, she was gone, the plain-faced librarian, mangled, crushed, *quaked*. How surprising, then, for Wanda to find herself, days later, missing the dead woman, missing telling her, "Good afternoon," then rhyming, "What you got in your snack bag today, Miss Poulée?"

The goat eating the book was Wanda's own fault, a result of her leaving the book in her bicycle basket and propping the bike against a chunk of cement at the side of the road while exploring the new public washrooms at Bishop Cove. The bicycle's kickstand was rusted through, since everything rusted on that island. The bike basket was woven of strips of pink plastic that had been scissored from a torn flap of shower curtain, and though she wasn't exactly proud of her inexpert handiwork, she liked the color. In America, where Wanda's mother worked as a maid for a family of four, the daughter and son were each given plug-in scissors to play with, scissors with brightly colored handles and serrated blades that cut the paper in motorized zigzags, but Wanda's scissors, or rather the household scissors, since they belonged to the household as much as to her, were ordinary rusty sewing scissors from which she'd thought to scrub the rust with a coconut husk, so as not to weave a basket engraved with rust stains. The new washroom was divided into equal halves, one for girls and one for boys, the doorways not yet marked for gender and between which you told the difference only by walking through one of them and finding Edmund Cupido's glorious male feet showing from under the door of a cubicle, at which point you hurried into the second half and sat down in the empty stall with a belly cramp you hoped was something far more gratifying than an ordinary stomachache, but no luck. The cement walls held matching chrome sinks under louvered window openings that were too high to see through to look at the cove. Small birds nested amid the louvers on one-half of the building, while on the other sill a lizard lay sunbathing. The faucets weren't yet rusted. There wasn't a mirror, but the water ran astonishingly fast from the tap in one-half of the washroom and then, after Edmund crossed the road to loiter in the parking lot outside the grocery store, it ran uncommonly warm from the tap in the other. The whole thing had been the generous gift of the Saint Veronica Master Conch Club, as was engraved on a plaque bolted to the wall. The Conch Club gave money for scholarships too. Wanda's Uncle Martin was a valet at the club, parking government limos for nineteen years. Everyone knew how good and generous the Conch Club was, until you took a minute to rest in your valet uniform on a bench in a rare cool breeze, got fired, and joined the other unemployed in the grocery store parking lot, where they nevertheless managed to look important.

THE BOLTS WEREN'T YET RUSTING but they would be soon. Both toilets flushed perfectly. There were several rolls of extra toilet paper on a shelf on the girls' side, but on the boys' side, no soap, since why bother with soap if boys never washed their hands? The soap on the girls' side would run out soon, so it was lovely, even if Wanda was disappointed by her belly cramp being not at all gratifying, to wash her hands in the soft, pink bubbles for a minute or two, a pink identical to that of the bicycle basket, as if the two objects shared a luminous essence, or, as the glorious Edmund Cupido might call it, "alumineth ethinth," since Edmund lisped. Queen Elizabeth the First had bathed only once a month, "whether I need it or not!" she had proudly exclaimed. Wanda dried her hands on her school uniform and then, noticing the paper towel dispenser for the first time, rinsed her hands all over again in order to dry them on one of those crisp paper towels, and then rinsed them a third time, since there were so many towels, and it was lovely to be in the presence of so much water gushing forth, when at home at the pump, all you got was a belch and a paltry cold trickle. And the water all around, and not only the mucky sewer of the brackish Bishop Cove but the open sea. She spun the faucet knob further and further around until it seemed the whole ocean sluiced over her knuckles, her fingers in thrall to what turned out to be the total unstoppability of the endlessly gushing water, since when she turned the knob back in the other direction, the water didn't stop coming but only swelled like a pudding, and when she spun the knob forward again, it came loose in her hand. Plus the thickened water turned suddenly dark, as if not from the sea but from between Wanda's legs in the rich, cleansing flow her mother had promised in one of many (but not enough) airmail letters, which she wrote during lulls (although there were no lulls) in her clothes ironing, silver polishing, and bed fluffing in the American house with the motorized serrated scissors and the ridiculous closets larger than houses. The other girl's mother kept pads in her daughter's clothes dresser, lying in wait for when pads were required, boxes of pads Wanda's mother arranged while laying out fresh rolls of paper in all the dressers, shelves, and cabinets, smoothing the paper with knuckly maid's fingers.

Soon the silty dark clots filled the little chrome sink and spilled onto the floor, pooling in places she wouldn't have noticed if not for their filling so thickly with fluid. The floor was cement. Her sticky sandals would warp in the heat the next day. She laid the twisted-off knob atop the paper towel dispenser, pulling out as many towels as she could with both hands and mopping the floor before stuffing a few up the faucet itself. But the tap kept gushing, so finally Wanda simply strolled out of there, her head aloft with pride as if the stream really were her own womanly flow, which was awfully late in coming, later than her own mother had promised, so late that Wanda nearly despaired of it happening, and she grandly waved the goat away from the basket of turned-over books on the tipped-over bike. The Good Queen lay in tatters, and the far more cherished *McGuffey's Third Eclectic Reader*, which was a gift to the library not from the Conch Club but from Wanda's own Sunday school class, lay in chewed-up pages here and there, the garlanded cover half-open, half-swallowed. *("Let me get my hat and cane and we will take a ramble." "Oh," said the man, laughing, "if you wish it, I will make some wheels for your horse. But mind, when it is finished, you must let me see it." But, you ask, why are they called hummingbirds? Whenever a word is imperfectly enunciated, the teacher should call attention to the sounds composing the spoken word. When you approach the spot where one of these birds has built its nest, it is necessary to be careful.*) It was a Roman-nosed goat, not even a pretty, dish-shaped one. Daintily it stepped along the stony beach, until it paused to tilt its face at Edmund Cupido, who stood across the potholed road in the parking lot at the grocery store, gazing with such purpose in Wanda's direction that all the other loiterers turned away. It was that afternoon that the earthquake struck. Just a miniature quake, as if only the library building, or the books themselves, or maybe only the librarian, appealed to it. Wanda's bicycle "thurvived," and so did the grocery store and the washroom. The goat and the pink bike basket were "thaved," as Edmund, years later, liked to remind her. And of the tumbled debris that was all that was left of the stout yellow library edifice, McGuffey's first, second, fourth, and fifth *Eclectic Reader*s were never seen again.

TAMARINDS

"You have elaborate penmanship," Cynthia told me in her funny but, to me, intoxicating speech, which made a whispery shriek like cracked clarinet reeds. The two of us were upstairs in the room called the Little Room, which I had wanted for my own but was Cynthia's now. With my brother, Sagistarius, whose real name was Spencer, I shared a much larger bedroom downstairs. It had its own bathroom and a walk-in closet that was larger by half than the Little Room, which was just a finished attic tucked into some eaves. A steeply slanted ceiling, scarred with peeling wallpaper, made the dormer room romantic in my eyes, as if somebody might waste away up there, cold but ecstatic. It wasn't cold, though; there was the same baseboard heating there as everywhere else. To reach a bathroom, Cynthia needed to cut through the playroom, go downstairs, duck past the gold-flecked guest bath in view of the chandelier in the dining room, and use the bathroom off the laundry room instead, where we shampooed Amy, our dog. Our mother had told me that she herself would wash there if she didn't have a dressing area all her own.

The window in the Little Room held a yellowed vinyl shade, and the rag rug appeared to have been paced back and forth on by somebody trapped in a starved, fitful reverie. Cynthia was to keep most of her clothing—the short-sleeved A-line uniforms, the church dress and hat, even her nightly washed underthings and some hosiery with reinforced toes, which she draped across the rung of a hanger to dry—next door in the playroom closet, alongside the old Hoover vacuum cleaner. The wire hanger would leave stains on her garter belt and bra, and her head would strike the ceiling whenever she got out of bed in the morning. She hung her nightgown on a hook from which also hung a mirror the size of a photograph. You had to draw aside the nightgown and breathe on the glass in order to write your name across the damaged sheen.

Things—bracelet charms, yo-yos—tended to become lost in the Little Room. Once, I was eating my snack up there and lost the spoon. Dannon yogurt was new in the US then; none of my school friends ate it yet. The fruit on the bottom was just like jam. I loved swirling the jam into the yogurt and putting my tongue to the heavy, tapered spoon before the swirling was done, taste-testing the gradual changes in flavor the more I stirred, the color deepening, the sour giving way to sweet . . . until at last I cheated, dipping into the final bubble of jam before stirring it in. But then, when I was finished, the spoon disappeared forever, leaving me feeling mighty and grave. That was how things went in the Little Room.

Nobody had ever complimented my penmanship before. Until then I thought of it only as handwriting, anyway.

"I won't be grading your handwriting," my tall, blonde schoolteacher had recently announced. Mrs. Higgins often scratched at her armpit while writing lessons on the chalkboard. Up went the hand wielding the stick of chalk, and in no time the opposite hand darted sideways to scratch at the nubbly underarm.

"You were born with your personality, therefore you can't help your handwriting!" I explained to my brother in Mrs. Higgins's chirpy manner, wearing imagined high-heeled pumps while I scribbled the words on an imaginary chalkboard, my hand scratching at my armpit as I stood on my toes to write the lesson. It was good of Sagistarius to let me be teacher, since I was such a careless student and earned such half-wit grades at school. He hadn't even turned ten yet, to my eleven, but of the many things I knew, the words and jokes and science lessons—like Latin for "October" was "eighth month," and bats pollinate flowers, and our new maid Cynthia's solar system was ten million four hundred light-years away—I'd learned most of them from him. I was his novice. He was my source, my guru.

Our mother poked her head in the playroom while I was putting the flourish on the *g*. A week later we discovered an actual chalkboard installed in the spot where the imaginary chalkboard once had been, with cartons of fresh chalk, a yardstick, two erasers, and a wooden desk. I didn't like our toy schoolroom nearly as much as I had loved our imagined one, which I missed much more than I missed that spoon, although it didn't seem lost, just one of many layers peeled away.

TAMARINDS

"Wanda her have intricate penmanship too. If you write her a note at the end of my letter, I send to she."

Later that day, I would try to convey these words to my brother using Cynthia's reedy speech, but my version of what the people at the agency called her "mixture of pidgin and Proper English" was totally inadequate. If I used "Proper English," in which, in the agency's memo, both *P* and *E* were capitalized, it sounded foolish and strained, but if I tried for the "pidgin," of which the *p* was lowercase, I got too many sounds wrong. I hoped to strike a balance, duplicating what our parents called our new maid's "patois," which in French, my brother taught me, meant "to clumsily paw."

Cynthia took a prim seat at the edge of the cot and tucked her skirt snugly around her legs, so as to make a taut surface on which to place the flimsy sheet of blue airmail stationery. When she finished her part of the letter, she handed it to me, along with a Bic. I shook the pen to make it bend. My brother was so full of tricks. Even when he was feeling under the weather, nothing ever stayed ordinary in his hands.

DEAR WANDA, I wrote in my most convoluted cursive.

Wanda, Cynthia's daughter, who was older than me by a couple of years, hoped to become a medical doctor. Her favorite food was bread pudding, which made Cynthia weep when she tried to describe it. Cynthia was already homesick that first day, for she hadn't come directly from her distant, rusty planet, which Sagistarius told me was called Saint Veronica, to our house on Long Island. Instead she had stopped at an even smaller planetoid to visit her aunts, and then she flew on to Queens to be trained for a week at the agency. When we

THE BELL AT THE END OF A ROPE

had first caught sight of her early that morning at Huntington Station, she was carrying a boxy brown suitcase along the raised metal footbridge spanning the tracks. Also a shiny black handbag, of which the clasp, since it was rusted, no longer worked. In the same hand she clutched a wad of tissue, which would turn out to be her most steadfast accessory.

"We're parked illegally," Mom remarked by way of saying she wouldn't be leaving the car to help Cynthia carry her cumbersome things, and, feeling sorry for our pathetic mother, since she was too shy even to greet her own maid at the train station, we too remained seated. Sagistarius had a sore throat anyway. Just then a new train rumbled under the footbridge, sending up a gust of air that lifted the skirt of Cynthia's uniform. Our mother blushed, since we could see the white garters, below the hems of a girdle, against Cynthia's skinny thighs. She had to plunk down the suitcase in order to push the handbag against the skirt. The suitcase popped open. More underthings tumbled into view, the wad of tissue dancing away like the ball that marked off song lyrics in cartoons. Since there were other colored ladies there at the station, all of them holding on to their hats, we weren't absolutely certain that this stick-figure one was Cynthia, but because of the suitcase and the sinewy arms, we were pretty sure it was. Plus, we'd seen a snapshot sent by the agency, the idea being we'd select a different maid if we were alarmed by the first one's appearance. The snapshot came with a personal history that our dad read aloud at the dinner table: "Completed Primary School; Married Age Eighteen. Employed at Church; Employed in Hotel Kitchen; Employed at Sister-in-Law's Tailoring Business. Does Not Drive. One Pre-teen Daughter. Husband in Cement."

We'd all laughed heartily at this last notation, and then finished our milk, rinsing down the joke before our new maid arrived.

Her eyes were yellow but her teeth were straight. By the time she was settled into our station wagon she was fully in tears, and her fresh wad of tissue, which had an unusual, glittery sheen like the softest sheet imaginable of fiberglass, seemed only to make her cry all the harder. As she blotted away and we were driving along through the prosperous streets of downtown Huntington, I asked her what she wanted us to call her.

"You don't want to be called Cookie?" I persisted when she had answered with surprise that she wished to be called Cynthia.

"No tanks," she said.

"Why would somebody named Cynthia want to be called Cookie?" our mother asked. Through her driving gloves I could count the lumps made by the rings Dad bought her for birthdays and anniversaries.

"No say," I answered in Spanish as my brother had taught me, and nuzzled closer against him on the big rear seat. I really grieved when he was sick. Even a splinter seemed to inch its way between us, clearing a narrow opening for wider breaches to follow. For this reason I was scared of his birthdays too, fearing he would surpass me and leave me behind. As if in mockery of my worries, he sneezed onto the window, thinking about how my belated graduation to chapter books wasn't paying off the way people expected. Aside from being only so-so at school, I tended to say and do regrettable things without the guile required to make them entertaining. Once,

THE BELL AT THE END OF A ROPE

I punched my best friend in the nose just to learn if I was brawny enough to cause pain, and another time I answered our babysitter, "Yes, Grandpa's finally out of the hospital," when the truth was he'd escaped only by having died there.

When we got home from the train station, Sagistarius headed straight for our walk-in closet to work on his model car, while I showed Cynthia up to the Little Room to watch her unpack and to tell her that for Sagistarius's birthday, I hoped she'd curl my hair. Cynthia replied that every year on *her* birthday a witch-friend of her mother's named Cora Hendrix, who hunted whelks for a living, left a bundle of the mollusks at their rickety door. There'd be the stomping of Cora's feet on the snail-studded landing (Cynthia stomped her feet on the floor in what we agreed was a lousy impression of the noise made by Cora's galoshes), after which, when you opened the door, you'd find a can of peas, a handful of whelks wrapped up in a fresh banana leaf, and tucked among them a sheet of lined paper so sodden that the words *Happy Birthday* had been all but rinsed away, leaving nothing but trickles of purple ink. And no sign of Cora anywhere. The can would be rusty, but because even zippers rusted from salt on Saint Veronica you ate the peas anyway. Since Cora was a witch, if you didn't eat the meals she brought you, you would regret it.

The items of interest to me in my new friend's suitcase were a photo of Wanda gnawing a stalk of sugarcane while wearing her Sandy Bay Primary School uniform, which had a Mary Jane collar fastened with a string bow tie; and Cynthia's husband's going-away gift to her, a toiletry kit featuring six foam hair curlers, a sea sponge, a bottle of Jergens, and, my favorite, a carton of the tingly, cruel-looking tissues, of which, a day later when the carton was opened, I would steal one to slip it under my pillow, like a book of spells you'd learn without needing to read it. We lined all these things up on the dresser my dad had assembled the week before. The dresser stood no higher than my hips but still got in the way of the door fully opening. My brother and I liked it a lot, mainly because we had never seen furniture made out of cardboard. Cynthia admired the plastic drawer pulls, which were attached with real screws. "The drapes they be laundered?" she asked hopefully, regarding the four bare panes of the window.

I told her you didn't need curtains in the Little Room because the window looked into the canopies of trees, which she seemed to agree with me were pretty to look at. Aside from my brother's tufted eyebrows, my favorite thing was climbing trees, though once I'd nearly slithered onto a chewed-up mouse staring blankly from the saddle of one of the trunks. Cynthia screeched when I told her about it, even though when she worked in the hotel kitchen she'd been required to clean the ink sacks from heaps of octopuses after yanking each animal inside out like a sock.

Finally I tugged at the window blind to show her how to keep the glare from waking her too early, but she said she rose every day before dawn anyway. Dawn happened in a flash on Saint Veronica, lasting nowhere near as long as our lazy pinkish hour. When she was my age, after mass she'd take the family bucket to fetch some water for washing, pound millet with a mortar, and hunt in ditches for their lost transistor radio. Then she'd walk past the governor's palace to school.

My envy over this account—palace! fetching water!—caused me to pull too hard on the window blind, which clattered onto the floor like a dropped roll of toilet paper. I had vacuumed the floor myself that morning, and spread fresh sheets on the cot, exchanging the blanket for one of stiff waffle weave. Having completed these tasks, I'd been paid my allowance, about which my mother forbade me to speak. Two dollars was more than Cynthia's husband earned in a day—plus the Little Room was probably a good deal more comfortable than Cynthia's whole house.

"Is it?" I asked as we rolled up the blind and tried unsuccessfully to hang it back in the window.

Cynthia answered simply that even though the cot wasn't nearly as lumpy as her mattress stuffed with old smocks on Saint Veronica, the room was not as comfortable because it wasn't her home.

"It is now," I said.

I realized this was cruel the minute I said it, which was how it always went with my social gaffes. Sagistarius had tried his best to train me not to make them, first in our imaginary classroom and then at the desk that had taken its place, but now that Cynthia was living right next to our playroom, it was in our walk-in closet where he took me to task.

I was dressing for bed when I told him what I'd said to her, for I always did tell him about my gaffes. Clothing dangled from their hangers and rods around us, pleating our bodies with serious shadows. How could I be so reckless? he asked, squatting amid the pouches of hardware, tubes of glue, sets of tweezers, and baggies of tires that came with the kit for his Vintage Monogram Big Deuce Ford Roadster. How could I be so careless as to tell our new maid, homesick as she was for her beloved birth-planet of Saint Veronica, floating light-years away in her longed-for galaxy, that Huntington, Long Island, was her home now?

"Especially when all her kids, such as they are, live *there*, not here?" he added, pointing at me with an axle in hopes it might turn lightbulbs on in my brain.

"Wanda's her only kid," I argued.

"In a certain way, that's true," he answered.

And then he told me that the rest of Cynthia's children, Wanda's many brothers, had all suffered the rotten luck of being changed into tamarinds on their tenth birthdays. It was the witch, Cora Henderson, who did it. Wanda was Cynthia's only kid who had made it past her tenth birthday and remained a human being. At least the tamarinds on Saint Veronica were animals, not fruits, but not monkeys either, Sagistarius explained, for they were not the chattery tamarind monkeys of other lands. No, on Saint Veronica the tamarinds napped amid vines and basked at the tops of canopies. They had moist, blunt, whiskery snouts, pale blue eyelids, and dopey but lovable temperaments.

"How big are they?" I asked.

"Koala-bear size. They have no voices. They're too hoarse. They can only rasp and wheeze and screech."

I feigned an indifferent disbelief, standing first on one foot, then the other, practicing my balance while stepping into my pajamas.

"That's impossible," I broached.

"Tell me why," said Sagistarius, his sore throat croaking unhappily. It seemed he truly wished to hear my wisdom on the subject. His nose was runny again so he wiped it on one of my nearby skirt hems and tucked the skirt amid the others like he was playing a prank.

"No say," I answered.

Sagistarius's chuckle heartened me.

DEPENDING ON WHERE YOU STOOD in our kitchen-dining area, you felt defined and contained by just one of the spaces, under its functional spell. In the kitchen you cooked, but in the dining room you were served. After some consideration those first few weeks, our mother elected for Cynthia's place to be set at the counter between the two spaces, where there stood some tall stools meant for after-school snacking. For dinners and family breakfasts, Cynthia was to perch on one of these stools. This meant that she would eat facing away from us, her back to our new Danish Modern dining table, her stick figure resisting the pull of gravity, her upraised elbows showing their dusting of cocoa, a placement she claimed to love.

Since our mother was such a good cook, Cynthia, at mealtimes, was only to assist. Sagistarius, with his head cold, had been excused from table setting for more days than I could count. The dog, Amy, trotted over to kiss him the second he sneezed, in order to keep his soul from escaping his body. I poured milk into tumblers and folded cloth napkins. Cynthia transferred the chicken to a platter, made a big salad, poured on too much dressing, sliced up a cantaloupe, and had time left over to scour the oven racks. Meanwhile, Mom whipped up gravy and related a funny story that Sagistarius and I had heard a million times: Friends of our parents once hired a maid and left her in the kitchen to prepare the cantaloupe. But she had never seen a melon before, and when she carried it out to the table, the fruit itself had been discarded so there were only the seeds, with their slippery fibers, heaped in the bowl.

Just as this story came to its rollicking close, Dad arrived home from the hospital, handed his doctor bag to the dog, to be delivered to the study, unknotted his tie, and for the second time that week slit open the airmail stationery containing Cynthia's letter to Wanda, which he had pulled absentmindedly out of the mailbox even though I'd been certain to prop up the flag. Cynthia burst into tears at the sight, and by the time we glued shut the torn flaps of blue paper and ran the letter back out to the mailbox, the rice had overcooked and the chicken was cold, the fat congealing into coins that slipped around in the gravy. When Cynthia was finished carrying the gravy boat chair to chair, she took her place at the counter to whisper her prayers, an act discernible only by a tremor beneath her hairnet, but no sooner had she started than the telephone rang, so up she jumped to answer it and take down a message. Unless it was Huntington Hospital calling with urgent news of Dad's patients, or Uncle Stanley in the midst of some crisis or other, like when Robert Kennedy got shot, our parents never took calls during meals. Uncle Stanley was crazy for Robert Kennedy, printing flyers for free at his print shop in Roslyn, then handing them out in shopping centers, his plump lips spitting into a megaphone. After the shooting he wept for days, phoning our parents whenever he felt the worst, wanting to punish them for grieving insufficiently.

Cynthia and I had learned about Kennedy before the rest of the household heard a thing about it, because the sewing machine had been moved from the basement up to the playroom so that Cynthia could sew the new dining room curtains in front of the TV. She always started her sewing exactly in time for "Break of Day" mass, and I joined her to help with the measuring and pinning, enjoying the way the chords of the mass, which, although it sounded out of tune to me since we were atheist Jews, lent a suffering air to the simple act of pinning, which was harder than it looked. It was warm up there in the playroom in June, which made Cynthia less homesick but not by much. Her sewing credentials were one of the reasons she had been "brought to New York," she confided half with pride and half abjectly. When she was at home, she went almost every morning to mass, but here she attended mass only on television. Just once, she'd asked permission to go on Sundays. Not meaning to put our mother on the spot, she made this request without me at her side, though I'd watched through the chink in the linen closet, which opened straight through the bookshelf over the dyed yellow tops of some forbidden paperbacks, which was a funny place to shelve them since we passed by them every day. There was *Soul on Ice*, *The Bad Seed*, *Black Like Me*, and *Naked Lunch*.

"Mrs. Trum I like to go to church on Sunday," Cynthia began while feather-dusting the andirons along the stout fireplace, so it was on the sooty feathers that our mother held her gaze.

"I know you do," she said from her reading chair, where she sat folding the *Long Islander* newspaper over a seam in the classifieds. "It said so in the notes the agency sent me. You must miss your church very much."

"I do, Mrs. Trum," Cynthia agreed.

"It's a shame you're such a help with our Sunday brunches," our mother said firmly. She was a bashful authority figure, and her self-conscious way of taking charge of her new employee was something she intended to overcome. To this end she had purchased a bell to be rung when she required our maid's immediate presence, a little handheld bell with the faintest clang. Cynthia would have needed to be already there in order to hear it, but she had a good ear, like certain moths, said Sagistarius. Our mother nodded her approval of the dusting of the andirons, and now crossed her feet on the ottoman and added, "The name is Thrumb, not Trum." Despite the smallness of her feet, her ankles were too broad.

"Trum," said Cynthia. "Before brunch maybe I go."

"*Ther-rum-bahh*," our mother enunciated.

"Thrumb," said Cynthia expertly when she and I were alone together. "This is very strange island where people they can't walk to church holding hand with their children or to market for fruit," she began, her brow pinched by the hairnet, her sympathy pluming to a secretive rage before collapsing again. There was never enough commotion here on Long Island. It wasn't natural for people to live so shut off from each other; even the neighbors were strangers to each other. Saint Veronica was such a cozy place to live that for people to say good-bye on the sidewalks would be like me, Linda, bidding a lofty farewell to Sagistarius every time he stepped into our walk-in closet, she exclaimed, alighting once more, like a bird on a feeder, on the subject of our closet, which was one of her favorite themes in her letters to Wanda. Wanda would admire the cars on Long Island, as would Cynthia's husband. Plus, he'd like the radios, only what use was music if nobody danced? To her, our country was "depress." It was good for me to learn that there were other ways of living than just driving to the supermarket once every week, hoping you might run into somebody who knew your mother's name while you were buying your salt and your pepper to spice up your food, she'd say, having already mourned the absence of whole nutmegs here, not to mention vanilla beans. On Saint Veronica, whole families gathered to play cards in rusty truck beds. You'd stroll along and there they'd be. But there was so much money here. Enough money to see Wanda through medical school. Cinnamons don't grow in jars, you know. Or coconuts in cans.

"That remind me," she concluded. "How many coconuts can one monkey him put in an empty sack?"

Mass being over, she bade me turn channels, searching in vain for our favorite cartoon, about a husband and wife who were forced, in hard times, to share a single bean for supper. But there was nothing but staticky throngs of serious-looking men dressed in mossy-looking suits. Channel upon channel, worried huddles of onlookers filled the screen. I turned the knob backward, then forward again, feeling, somehow, even though I had received no letter from her, just how I imagined Wanda must feel; loyal, in thrall to her mother's resentful bursts of giddiness (I'd even started doing better in those final weeks at school, completing some of my homework and raising my hand to answer, correctly sometimes, a few of Mrs. Higgins's questions), and maybe even a little jealous of her brothers, who were tamarinds rather than schoolchildren now and so got to climb around in trees, picking berries as they went or simply plucking off leaves and watching them spiral into the greenery, the twisting branches like the cages of amusement park rides whirling and spinning, sky below, earth above, everything topsy-turvy up there.

When the camera turned to some footage of Mrs. Ethel Robert Kennedy, Cynthia betrayed a flicker of interest, her eyes veering away from the twist of blue thread as it spooled around the bobbin. Somehow over the next half hour, the curtain lining was in place, the panels draped flatly over the ironing board, the blue so rich we could smell the dyes, my pins regular only in their unevenness.

How many coconuts can one monkey him put in an empty sack? I asked myself for days, failing two school quizzes as a result and even drawing a picture of the coconut sack on the stall in the girls' room, unable to draw the monkey itself. At last I took the riddle to Sagistarius, who often solved them at once, although sometimes days went by before he ventured his guess. Cynthia didn't like that he solved them, feeling, logically it seemed, that his answers reduced them, the way I felt about the classroom in our playroom. For this reason, she posed trickier riddles as time went on.

Still, "Umbrella," he might venture, while we walked to the bus stop one rainy morning. *My father has a house that stands on one post.*

"A pot on a flame." *The black one him squatting, the red one him licking his bottom.*

"Leaves." *We tread on the dead, they answer. We tread on the living, they do not answer.*

They all seemed too hard even after he'd solved them, and anyway I doubted monkeys lived on Saint Veronica or in any other galaxies. I wondered if the sacks were burlap, like for the races at school. Sack races always earned me my only Field Day ribbons, probably as a result of my submerged intellect's low center of gravity, Sagistarius reasoned. Distracted by such trains of thought, I'd find myself looping away from Cynthia's riddles before trudging helplessly back again, all ideas in a jumble. "Why does the dog she sleep in the fireplace when it thunder outside?" Cynthia might ask, the splintered chimes of her English swinging from their rigid threads, and for a minute or two I'd be totally stumped, thinking, "Dog? Fireplace?" supposing it was a riddle she posed.

"Cynthia-perhaps-the-curtains-will-be-hung-tomorrow-evening," our mother said while caressing her fork, the topaz winking on her finger, the opal ablaze. Because of Kennedy's funeral procession, the TV was on in the knotty pine chest near the dining room table, though our mother found all news unappetizing.

Cynthia-it-appears-that-the-silver-needs-polishing.

Cynthia-it-appears-that-the-reason-for-the-dryer-not-functioning-properly-is-that-the-lint-has-not-been-cleared.

Cynthia swiveled away from her dinner to show she had heard, and then turned back to her view of the glass oven door, in which the hearse was reflected. During the footage of the rare nighttime burial, the mourners ghostly on the humid grass, my brother finally ventured—his hoarseness turned to laryngitis, his damp nose plumper than before—"One coconut."

Cynthia shrugged, demoralized, while Dad tilted his head in puzzlement, not having heard of our riddles at all.

"After one," rasped Sagistarius, "the sack it is no longer empty."

TAMARINDS

THE LITTLE HANDHELD BELL gave its faintest clang from the living room late one day, a sound like two paper clips mating, Sagistarius liked to say. "Cynthia-somebody's-at-the-door-please!" Mom called feebly.

We were up in the Little Room, Cynthia and I, looking for her eyeglasses, which she had propped on the cardboard dresser for just two minutes while putting curlers in my hair in honor of the next day being Sagistarius's tenth birthday. Mom never did my hair. She didn't know how. I reveled in the way it tickled my spine to have my hair combed and parted, the press of the eaves bearing down on this act to make it more significant, the room smelling of Cynthia's Jergens hand lotion and her dusky scent of melanin. The eyeglasses weren't in the cardboard drawers nor caught in the squares of the waffle-weave blanket, and when we looked in the wall sconce, all that we found was the go-go boot charm from my friend Lucy's bracelet, which I had long since given up searching for.

Cynthia went downstairs to the door, where the knocking had turned to kicking and banging.

"Who is it?" Mom asked, tilting forward in her chair but only for a moment, overcome by her ample bottom and thirty-one-inch waist, symbols, to me, of her natural reserve, her due elegance, and her lifelong distaste for physical activity.

I rode a couch cushion downstairs toboggan-style to where Cynthia stood in the open doorway, facing into the stillness, weeping onto some object she held in her hands. It wasn't a sorrowful weeping this time, but one of her giddy, hiccupy sobs, her shoulders quaking with glee, the stockings wrinkling at her ankles. Aside from the regicide, nothing exciting had happened on this planet for months, and like me she seemed glad for tonight's interruption, no matter what it portended. Our house was too even tempered, our parents never fought or argued, no monsoons leaked through our bedroom ceilings, no rust bloomed in the bathroom sinks, even the gruesome bullfight tapestry hung becalmed in our parents' living room.

At first glance, the view past the threshold appeared disappointingly ordinary—some swells of moist grass, the rows of whitewashed stones, nearly phosphorescent, flanking the driveway—until you saw that the storm door had been kicked in and that beyond the shattered glass, amid our dad's dwarf maples, lay the many scattered parts of Sagistarius's Vintage Monogram Big Deuce Ford Roadster, which he had finished detailing just a day or two before.

Aside from a scratch on the stock-grille insert, the car had been perfect. The bucket seats shone and the headlights blinked. It rolled decisively around with barely a nudge, and took the foremost place among its less impressive forebears on the shelf above our beds.

But now here it lay, murdered.

Even the cops, who arrived in just minutes, agreed that the car had been painstakingly eviscerated, not just impulsively stomped apart. Somebody—not Billy Webb, the neighbor boy who hated Sagistarius but was off on a class trip to Mystic Seaport—had dismantled the roadster piece by piece and strung the innards here and there in deepening twilight amid the not yet crimson maple leaves. The steering wheel cartwheeled off one of the branches, while the gently swinging bulb of the gearshift knob made me think of the chewed mouse I'd found in our woods. There was something sly about this "car-nage," as Sagistarius bravely called it, unable to speak above the hoarsest of whispers. Dazed, docile, he slid near me on the love seat, feverish still, tugging thickly at his eyebrows. Nearby stood our dad with the uniformed men and their paddle-shaped clipboards, Mom so agitated that she needed to be fed sips of water from a cup I'd fetched her. Cynthia perched in forlorn uprightness, her starched uniform stiffly cylindrical around the rod of her posture, her wet lashes clumped in Vs, the redness of her eyes more apparent than usual due to the missing eyeglasses. Her hands lay folded in her lap (for once she held no tissue) after handing me the item at which she had been squinting when I'd found her at the door, a piece of lined paper, now scrunched into a ball. Amazed that someone might sit so tall as Cynthia yet still appear to be shielding something, I wedged the wad of paper tight between my knees in an effort to look that way myself, hair curlers and all.

We'd been eating tongue for dinner that evening, the sour fragrance of the meat perplexing the cops, who'd never smelled it before or bitten into a slice of the bright-pink muscle (the taste buds spitted when you chewed them). Beyond the doorway to the kitchen could be seen the hulking shape of the deli-style meat slicer with its giant metal blade, from which Cynthia always recoiled, although no other sharp objects frightened her. She especially liked the larding needle, which she had learned how to use when she was a teen in the hotel kitchen, and though she felt no nostalgia for those hectic, steamy evenings, she'd met her husband-to-be on the hotel grounds—before he was in cement, I said to myself whenever I thought of that part of her history.

"So the doorbell rang and then the knocking began? Or did the knocking come first?" asked one of the cops.

Sagistarius squirmed. He was often sheepish, but for their sakes, not his own, when self-important people made numbskulls of themselves.

"Has there been a dispute in the neighborhood lately? A business or property issue? Has your family made enemies? The dog didn't bark?"

"She's too polite," I answered, and then our mother blushed and added, "Cynthia-the-slicer-requires-regular-sponging-please."

Cynthia flinched and rose for the kitchen, and for the first time it was clear to me that the reason for the whiteness of her uniform was to emphasize the blackness of her legs and arms. And how ropey they were with hunger for her lost, changed sons, who only nibbled their breakfast rolls side to side, as if playing harmonicas, before scampering back into the trees to play. I wondered if Wanda felt torn, like I would, praying on the one hand to remain a human girl but on the other hand to join them amid the scrabble of vines between the weird mirror image of ground and sky.

"Boyfriend?" asked the cop, tipping his pencil in the direction of the kitchen.

Mom went totally blank.

"Not that we know of," Dad replied.

More glass fell out of the kicked-in door and crashed onto the stoop. Mom blushed more deeply, sipping her water. For a moment she considered me and my brother. Should we be requested to leave the room too? We were used to this in her. She was a prudish conversationalist. Many seemingly

TAMARINDS

harmless topics embarrassed her. For her sake alone, I dreaded life's milestones: the day I would need my first tampon, for example, and Sagistarius's move to the guest room down the hall so we wouldn't need to share. Our first underarm hair might kill her, we thought.

"We *have* noticed a certain amount of . . . the Bay Club had prohibitions until Harry Chapin made a point of . . . even though he wasn't exactly . . . as far as we know," Mom stammered, caressing the chair arm just as she soothed the desktops at parent-teacher night at school or comforted the plate rim at dinnertime, the gemstones glinting as she petted, her middle finger tracing circles on glass or upholstery, the other fingers upraised, the whole arm trembling.

"I lost my shoes once at the Bay Club," offered one of the cops. "I jumped off the dock and when I swam to the beach they were sunk, but then at high tide they washed up again."

"And Mrs. McGowan in the house with the tall white pillars arrived here from Germany as a young woman," Mom added demurely

We waited for the rest, except there wasn't any more. Not even Sagistarius managed to decipher this vague, blushing speech of our mother's, although we knew right away that the reason for the maid being sent to sponge the slicer was to keep her from hearing this along with the rest of us. Watching Cynthia pulling on rubber gloves, I smoothed the crumpled ball of paper open on my lap, not entirely surprised to find the witch Cora Henderson's spell bleeding across it: HAPPY TENTH BIRTHDAY SPENCER.

"What's that?" my brother whispered, his eyelids pale blue beneath the hooded brows.

Earlier that day, while lounging sideways on my bed with one arm tingling under my pillow, where I held the sheet of glittery, spell-like tissue paper, I had whispered, "Farewell, changling," as he stepped into our closet, but only now did he gape at me, horrified.

"No say," I answered, but I let him take my hand. Our future was upon us.

ABOUT THE AUTHOR

Abby Frucht's first story collection was *Fruit of the Month,* for which she received the Iowa Short Fiction Prize in 1987. Since then she has published five novels—*Snap* (Ticknor & Fields); *Licorice* (Graywolf); *Are You Mine?* (Grove/Atlantic); *Life before Death* (Scribner)—all of which will soon be released as eBooks from Dzanc Books' rEprint Series—and *Polly's Ghost* (Scribner). A recipient of a Best of the Web Award, Frucht has served for many years as a mentor and advisor at Vermont College of Fine Arts and is writing a novel with her colleague Laurie Alberts. She lives in Wisconsin and has two grown sons.

We hope you enjoyed
Abby Frucht's *The Bell at the End of a Rope.*

Please visit us at NARRATIVEMAGAZINE.COM
for more Narrative Library books.

Made in the USA
Charleston, SC
11 September 2012